Christopher Tull was born in 1936, the son of a country rector. Ordained in 1962, he spent all of his ministry in parishes in rural Devon. Now retired, he still lives in Devon and remains active in church life. Although the characters in his stories are fictitious, much of the inspiration for them comes from the many wonderful people he has been privileged to know, both in his early life and in the course of his work. His books show how rural churches can be alive and active today, with all the joys and sorrows, traumas and fun that take place within them. He has never forgotten the important part that faith and prayer play in all of this.

To Mayard.

FOR EVER IN GREEN PASTURES

Christopher Tull

With my good wishes

Chris Tull

Broad **S**treet **P**ublishing

Printed and bound in Great Britain by
Short Run Press Limited, Exeter

BROAD STREET PUBLISHING
Arden Cottage, Coombeshead Road, Highweek,
Newton Abbot TQ12 1PZ
Tel +44 (0)1626 365478

Dedicated to all the clergy and lay people who
continue to keep the flame of faith burning bright in the
small country churches of our land

* *

I would also like to express deep appreciation to
Jiff Villiers for kindly allowing me to reproduce
watercolours from her book
To Stand and Stare

To Norman Dallyn
who helped me with my word processing

To Chrissie and Mark Young of
Broad Street Publishing for their help
and dedication to publishing my books

And last, but not least, to my wife, Rosemary, who
checked my work and came up with good
ideas when I most needed them

Acknowledgements

Weep if you Must
by
Joyce Grenfell

The Better Plan
by
William Weeks
reproduced courtesy of
Peninsula Press

Contents

For Ever in Green Pastures

This is Christopher Tull's fourth book.
Set between 1980 and 1986, his stories paint a
hilarious, poignant and thought-provoking portrait of
rural life with the church at the heart of the community.

* *

Jack and Mary Longfield live in the truly rural
West Country parish of Ashenridge. Jack has been rector
of the church there for some twenty five years and has
five other rural parishes in his care, Westaleigh,
Brookworthy, North and South Monkton, and
the smallest of them all, Combe Peter.
Jack and Mary have been sharing ideas about moving
to pastures new, even retirement, but when the
Bishop of Whiteminster unexpectedly announces he is
planning to close all of Jack's churches bar one,
life takes a very different turn.

Chapter 1

The Unwelcome Letter

The letter I'd really dreaded arrived in that morning's post. I picked it up and endeavoured to open it, but my hands were shaking so badly I found myself unable to perform that simple task. I'd been expecting the letter for days, yet now it had arrived I could do nothing but hold it in my trembling hands. How I wished my dear wife, Mary, was here with me, but she'd already left for a morning's shopping in Leighford and wouldn't be home until lunchtime.

I made my way into the study. A copy of the parish magazine, the Badger News, lay on my desk, the six churches of Ashenridge, Westaleigh, North and South Monkton, Brookworthy, and the smallest of them, Combe Peter, all portrayed on the front cover.

I glanced at the envelope again. Postmarked 'Whiteminster' and dated the 14 July 1980, the address was in the blue typescript I instantly recognised as that of the bishop's secretary. Over the years I'd received many letters addressed in the same way. None, however, had been quite as important as this one. On it hung not only the future of the parishes I had served for nearly a quarter of a century, but also how I might spend the rest of my working life.

* *

At the beginning of June I'd received a call from the Bishop of Whiteminster's secretary which had sounded so promising.

"The bishop has heard about your work and is keen to meet with you and your parishioners. He would very much like to preach at your Communion Service on the 29th June."

As the bishop had only recently been installed I felt honoured that he wanted to visit us so soon. I could not have anticipated the reason for his visit.

Ashenridge Church had been packed that Sunday with parishioners from all six churches coming together for such a special occasion. The bishop had beamed with delight at the congregation and their expectant faces. He spoke fondly of churches such as Ashenridge becoming like shining beacons in his diocese. If only he'd left it at that. Not so. He went on to say how he intended achieving this – by reducing the three hundred struggling rural churches in his diocese to a mere fifty flourishing ones, of which Ashenridge would be a fine example.

Imagine how much fund raising it would save. With fewer clergy to pay and many decaying buildings no longer needing maintenance, the diocese would at last be put on a firm financial footing. More revenue would come from selling off redundant rectories, possibly even the churches themselves. In future, the rector of Ashenridge would take just one combined Sunday service for all six parishes.

The bishop's face had remained radiant throughout. He was totally unaware of the shocking impact his words were having on those gathered before him. I glanced at Tim Ashman, our team vicar, and Will Swift, our highly-respected lay reader, and could only guess at what was going through their minds.

The bishop was still smiling blissfully as he sailed over to the village hall where the churchwarden, Annie Cook, had prepared some light refreshments. He could only spare a few minutes to meet with the congregation before charging off to another appointment.

Few joined in. Hardly anyone spoke to him. Those who did simply made polite conversation. Others huddled in small groups giving vent to their feelings, feelings they dared not express to the bishop's face. I could see that Tim was about to give the bishop a piece of his mind, but I restrained him saying this was neither the time nor the place. A stony-faced Will Swift remained silent.

Out of courtesy I thanked the bishop for coming to Ashenridge and for sharing with us his vision for the future. I was sure everyone found his ideas interesting but he must appreciate that if we said little it was because it had all come as a bit of a surprise. As he turned to leave the hall we quickly shook hands and I promised a letter would be sent to him once the parishes had had time to discuss his 'vision for the future'.

Over the next few days the rectory telephone seemed to ring non-stop. The congregation may have been reluctant to voice their feelings directly to the bishop, but Mary and I now took the full brunt of everyone's anger. Their message was loud and clear. The bishop had to be stopped and it was up to me to do it.

Working on the basis that three heads are better than one, Tim, Will and I joined forces and agreed that the situation was serious enough to go on the offensive. It was Will who summed things up. "The time for pussyfooting's over. We have to let the bishop know we mean business."

After much soul searching I put pen to paper, and I did not mince my words.

So here I was, some two weeks later, staring at a harmless-looking envelope, praying the bishop had had second thoughts. Perhaps he'd understood the dramatic affect his words had had on the congregation. What if something had happened over the last few days to make him change his mind? Had my letter persuaded him not to make any hasty decisions? After all, in that same letter I'd had to inform him that Tim Ashman would be leaving to take up a new post. Not only had I told him of Tim's imminent departure, I'd added that I knew of an excellent replacement, an enthusiastic young man who was in tune with rural life and keen to work with me.

There was nothing for it. I ripped open the envelope and started reading.

'*My dear Jack…*' I skipped the first few lines of pleasantries and got to the main point of his letter. '*I've considered the facts you raised in your letter, and whilst I appreciate your remarkable achievements, times are changing, and not only here in the West Country…*

'*I do urge you and your parishioners to share my vision for the future. As I've said before, your church at Ashenridge will become one of the shining beacons in the diocese.*

'*The burden of caring for six parishes will be lifted from your shoulders, and although I was sorry to learn that Tim Ashman will be leaving Westaleigh, it seems rather providential that his departure fits in with my plans. Naturally there will be no need for you to seek a replacement…*'

Everything I'd feared was coming true – closure and centralisation. I'd heard this kind of talk dozens of times. Bishops, archdeacons, town-bred clergy, all had harped on the same tune but failed to see that it would leave many people without a church of their own.

To country folk the church is the centre of their community. Worshippers from the surrounding parishes might pour into Ashenridge Church for special occasions, as indeed they had for the bishop's visit, but they most certainly would not for their normal Sunday service, which they would expect to take place in their own parish church. Deep down I knew that, once closed, most of them would consider the doors to the kingdom of heaven firmly shut. This twentieth-century policy of closing churches had been dressed up as progress, but the exact opposite was the truth.

I paced round the garden gripping the letter. Had I misread it? Had the bishop's secretary omitted some important word that might have reversed the situation? I read it again. There could be no doubting the bishop's message, and although I had foreseen a distant day when one clergyman would be expected to serve all six churches, I had not expected it to happen so soon.

I felt like tearing his wretched letter into shreds. Instead I walked the short distance from the rectory to the church. Thank God it was empty. With tears streaming down my face I prayed for guidance. The Bible lay open on the lectern and through a blur of tears I read the verse before me: 'As I was with Moses, so shall I be with thee. I will not fail thee'. I returned to the rectory with those words ringing in my ears.

All round me the hilltops were bathed in glorious sunlight. Hope seemed to be everywhere and with it the power of God.

* *

For months Mary and I had been talking about the possibility of moving to pastures new and making way for a younger man. But if Moses could keep going until he was well over a hundred why couldn't I, at half his age, do the same? The faces of the people I had loved and served for so long appeared before me. What right had I to abandon them to an uncertain future?

Without realising it, the bishop had laid down a challenge. I could either walk away or take up that challenge. In an instant I knew what I must do.

The Bishop of Whiteminster might look upon Ashenridge as a shining beacon in his diocese as much as he liked, but I would do everything in my power to prevent him extinguishing the lights at my other churches.

For the foreseeable future Mary and I would be putting our plans on hold. We would not be leaving Ashenridge.

Chapter 2

An Urgent Need

It was a beautiful August morning. Following a glorious sunrise the surrounding hills were bathed in a pastel-pink light and everything seemed still.

For once I had nearly the whole morning free. I'd take my usual stroll down to Radd's, fetch the newspaper, have breakfast with Mary, and then we'd spend a few hours together in the garden which, following a wet spell, had become sadly overgrown. With the departure of Tim Ashman days like these were few and far between.

As I neared the village shop Ernie Rudge flew past almost knocking me to the ground. With a brief 'sorry' he made for his van. Tyres screeching, he drove off like a bat out of hell. I could have sworn he had tears in his eyes.

I went into the shop hoping for some sort of an explanation, but Mrs Radd was busy at the post office counter, Mr Radd was nowhere to be seen, and their shop assistant was hardly the right person to ask.

Perhaps Mary could throw some light on it, but no, she'd heard nothing untoward.

Try as I might I could not concentrate on reading the newspaper. There was nothing for it. I put the paper down and told Mary I'd have to drive over to Ernie's to see if I could be of any help. I'd been hoping for a free morning. The last thing I wanted was an urgent problem. Then I felt ashamed for thinking like that. Jesus put others first and I must do the same, no matter what pressures I faced.

Poor Ernie. Only a year ago I'd laid his wife to rest in Brookworthy churchyard. Since then I'd visited him on several occasions, but if truth be told he was finding it hard coming to terms with Maud's death. On one of my visits we chatted about hobbies and it transpired that as a youngster he'd loved stamp collecting. I too had been a collector for most of my adult life and it wasn't difficult to persuade Ernie to renew his hobby. He got himself an album with a picture of a Penny Black on the cover and on a recent visit he'd insisted on lending it to me, but I'd been so busy I hadn't got round to looking at it.

This gave me the perfect excuse to pay Ernie another visit and, grabbing the album from the bookshelf, I hurried to the front door. As I went to open it the bell started ringing. It was Annie Cook, her crooked finger poised ready to press the bell again.

Over the years Annie had become a good friend, but she always spoke her mind and had something of a sharp tongue.

"Well, well," she said, spotting the album and looking at me as though I were a naughty child playing with toys when I should have been in school. Then, seeing Ernie's name written in huge letters on the cover she added: "I know how busy you are so I'll take that for you. I'll probably be seeing Ernie tomorrow." With that she made a grab for the album.

"No, no, Annie," I said firmly. "Thanks for the offer, but I want to return it myself."

Annie shrugged. "Suit yourself. In any case I came to see you about something far more important. As churchwarden I thought you should know the cleaners are threatening to walk out because hymn books are being left all over the place instead of being handed in at the end of the service."

"Annie, why does nobody listen? I keep on telling you, it's the responsibility of those who hand out the hymn books at the beginning of a service to make sure they are put away at the end. It's as simple as that."

In the past Len Cooksley would have tidied away any books left lying around without making a fuss, but the onset of 'arthuritis' had forced him to relinquish his job as sexton. How I missed him, his unflinching willingness to help and, above all, his eccentric way with words that could have you laughing until your sides ached.

"Never mind the hymn books," Annie continued, seeing danger in my eyes. "Come to think of it I saw Ernie driving through the village earlier on. I've never seen a man look so miserable. I should hardly think he'd be in the mood to talk to you about philately."

Neither of us had heard Len Cooksley approaching and suddenly there were three of us squeezed together on the rectory doorstep.

"What's that you'm sayin' about Phil 'Attersly? Cor, I remembers 'im from years back. Lived over South Monkton way. Nice old boy. You'd remember 'im, rector. 'Ad a dreadful haccident with 'is tractor. 'Twas in all they newspapers. Walked with a stick after that." Here Len waved his own stick in the air. "Reckon 'e'd be dead by now."

With that Len spotted the album and leaned across Annie to get a better look at the picture on the cover. "Who's that then, rector?"

Before I had a chance to answer Annie declared authoritatively: "That's a Penny Black."

Len winked at me over the top of Annie's head. "Penny Black? You'm pulling my leg, Annie. Don't recognise 'er from round 'ere!"

We were now interrupted by the arrival of Jonathan Hopkins. Jonathan was the 'between jobs' clergyman foisted on me by the bishop. An insignificant-looking man in his mid-forties, his spikey brown hair, a tendency to scuttle everywhere and repeatedly snuffle put me in mind of a giant hedgehog. He spoke with such an air of authority on any matter regarding the church few would realise he'd only recently been ordained.

The bishop had sent Jonathan to assist me for a few hours each week, which I suspected was his way of acknowledging I could not cope on my own. I'd heard along the grapevine he'd had to backtrack on his 'vision for the future', but I was going to need a lot more help than a few hours each week to give all six parishes in the Badger Group the attention they deserved.

It was Jonathan's turn to scrutinise the album, and through his snuffles he exclaimed: "I'm so sorry. Please don't let me spoil your fun. I had no idea you were taking time off today."

This was all getting too much for me. "I am not taking time off," I said rather testily. "Just because I'm holding this album does not mean I've abandoned my work."

Ignoring me, and snuffling again, Jonathan continued: "Only I well remember what you said about the importance of taking a break if things started getting on top of you."

"No, Jonathan," I assured him. "Things are not getting on top of me and I have a perfectly good reason for holding this album. Now, if you'll excuse me."

Thankfully Annie took this as her cue to leave, but not before firing one more shot about the cleaners and the untidy hymn books.

A smug grin appeared on Jonathan's face. "Dear, oh dear," he snuffled. "Sounds like trouble brewing."

With that Annie and Len turned to leave and as they walked down the drive I overheard Len muttering: "Poor rector, gets 'imself in a bit of a flummox these days. And as for that 'Opkins. Wish someone would tell 'im to blow 'is flippin' nose!"

I pulled the front door firmly shut and jangled the car keys. Thankfully Jonathan took the hint and scuttled after Annie and Len.

I got into the car, placed the album on the passenger seat, and had almost reached the bottom of the drive when a Land Rover pulled up. My heart sank. It was Peter Eastridge, whose ruddy complexion and pronounced nose, along with a crest-like tuft on the top of his head, reminded me of a cross cockatoo.

Peter had been a thorn in my side for more than twenty years. It went back to the 1950s when, following the death of his father, he'd assumed he'd step in as churchwarden. When the vote had gone against him he blamed me. But two years ago his dream of becoming a churchwarden had come true and since then our relationship had improved. He no longer used the scathing expression 'fine rector us's got', and strangely enough the bishop's bombshell had brought the two of us together in a way probably nothing else would.

"Rector, I'm glad you'm 'ere. I tried ringin' you three times last night, but there's never anyone 'ome to answer the 'phone. 'Tis just that you'd best come over to the church to see for yerself. Four slates are a bit loose over the porch and it may get wet inside and bring the plaster down."

I followed Peter wondering if I'd ever be free from having to dot every 'i' and cross every 't' when it came to even the smallest of matters concerning Ashenridge Church. The slates had certainly come loose, but there was no risk of them falling, and they hardly warranted my immediate attention.

The church clock struck eleven. Any chance of driving over to Ernie's now was out of the question because I was due to attend a working lunch at the archdeacon's house in Whiteminster. I quickly promised Peter I'd get someone in to look at the slates and drove off thinking, yet again, I was letting poor Ernie down.

* *

I was the last to arrive at Whiteminster. I had barely got one foot out of the car when the archdeacon appeared. "Good to see you, Jack." He started chuckling. "So that's how you fill your time." He'd spotted Ernie's album resting on the passenger seat. I felt rather guilty for thinking it, but Ernie Rudge's album was causing me quite a lot of trouble.

It so happened I was sitting next to the archdeacon at lunch and after he'd said grace I found myself staring at a bookcase crammed full of stamp collecting magazines. The archdeacon smiled at me. "Wonderful hobby, Jack. Keeps me sane too."

Following lunch an official had been invited to give a talk on the importance of insuring church buildings. The room was unbearably hot, my head was throbbing, and as the speaker's voice droned on the reproachful face of a dying Ernie kept flashing before me. Luckily, the archdeacon recognised my anxiety and assured me I would not cause offence by leaving early.

* *

I'd so looked forward to working in the garden with Mary, and I always enjoyed the archdeacon's lunch. They should have been the bright spots of my day. But I had to acknowledge that, sadly, there were few 'bright spots' at all these days.

Although the bishop had come to understand it was not entirely in his province to close or sell off redundant churches, my workload continued to grow rather than shrink, and although Jonathan Hopkins had provided some help, I realised his few hours a week in Ashenridge would not last for ever.

Mary had frequently mentioned that these days I seemed to be turning every problem into a crisis, and I knew she was right. Lack of sleep and constant worrying left me feeling dog tired, as a result of which I just wasn't coping.

Chapter 3

Man's Best Friend

As I drove home from the archdeacon's I became more and more frustrated. The road from Whiteminster to Ashenridge is certainly beautiful, but it is also narrow and full of twists and turns as it follows the bends of the River Badger. It only takes one slow vehicle to create a tailback. One can understand if it's a tractor or heavy lorry, but on this occasion it was a blue Mini being driven in the middle of the road making it almost impossible for anyone to overtake.

A few vehicles managed to get past, but not without the screeching of brakes and a lot of hooting from oncoming cars. If only the Mini would pull over, but it didn't. I gave a gentle toot then a longer and louder one. The Mini continued at 25mph. The road became clear and I grabbed the opportunity to get past. As I overtook the driver gave a long blast of indignation on his horn.

It was approaching four o'clock when I arrived back in Ashenridge. If I hurried I'd still have time to visit Ernie before the five o'clock confirmation class.

I looked in at the rectory to warn Mary I might be running a bit late for the class. She was not alone and I found myself being confronted by Ashenridge's church treasurer, the formidable Mrs Mathilda Pink, who wished to discuss a serious matter. The money from various church collections had been added up incorrectly. I was quick to point out that I never handled the money, but for some reason Mrs Pink felt I was to blame and insisted I make enquiries. As she left the first of the confirmation candidates arrived. Once again I was trapped.

"I've got one piece of news for you," Mary said as I sat down for a hurried tea. "During your confirmation class Annie rang to say she'd seen Ernie Rudge this afternoon. He was in Radd's holding forth about some hooligan drivers overtaking him on his way back from Whiteminster. He thought one of them was you."

"Not me," I replied indignantly. "I never passed him. I'd know his van anywhere."

"But he wasn't in his van. Annie said his van is in for a service, and the garage in Whiteminster lent him a blue Mini. Why he goes all that way for repairs heaven knows. Anyway, I think you can safely leave seeing him until tomorrow."

This was a relief as I had a Church Council meeting at Combe Peter later that evening which was sure to go on for ages.

Despite Mary's comforting words I was still concerned about Ernie and hardly got a wink's sleep. The following morning, ignoring my dear wife's protestations, I skipped breakfast so that I could make an early start.

Ernie's cottage sat behind a neatly cut hedge and as I drew up I noticed a blue Mini parked in the lean-to where Ernie normally kept his van. From somewhere inside a radio was blaring out pop music. To my relief he appeared at his front door, very much alive and dancing to the music like a two-year-old.

"Come on in, come on in, Mr Longfield," he said, beaming all over his face. "I won't keep you a minute."

I could hear the sound of excited barking and with that Bess came running out to greet me, her tail wagging nineteen to the dozen.

"It's a miracle," Ernie choked through his tears of joy. In his hands he held a bottle of stout and two large tumblers. "I tell you, I thought she was a gonner."

As Ernie poured the stout I tried to get him to explain. It was hard work shouting against the ear-splitting music. His answers came in excited bursts as he yelled above the radio. Then I resorted to my trick of speaking so quietly that he could not hear me without turning the volume down. His story went something like this.

In the past Ernie had always kept a dog, strictly for rounding up sheep. When cute little Bess came along his wife, Maud, had seen things differently. She allowed her into the house, gave her choice titbits, generally fussed over her. Ernie had had little patience with any of this, but since Maud's death everything had changed. Ernie saw Bess in a new light. She somehow took the place of his wife, someone to talk to, to make the house feel alive, to greet him when he came home.

When Bess started losing weight Ernie pretended not to notice, but each day Bess became less and less interested in her food. She'd even snapped at him when he attempted to stroke her head. In the end he had to admit something was seriously wrong. He tried tempting her with the very best of dog food, but that didn't work. He delayed taking Bess to the vet for fear of what he might be told. What a terrible betrayal if she had to be put down.

Then a few days ago the fishmonger had called and was horrified to see Bess lying lifeless in her basket. He all but accused Ernie of mistreating Bess.

"That's when you saw me in the village, rector," Ernie continued. "I'm sorry I nearly knocked you over, but I hardly knew what I was doing. I'd just made up my mind to take Bess to the vet.

"Everything seemed to go against me. The van started playing up, I arrived late for the appointment and the vet had already been called out on an emergency. All I could do was leave Bess with the vet's wife. She was very kind and told me not to worry, but I still did.

"Then the van had to be checked over at the garage in Whiteminster. They lent me a Mini, but I'd never driven a car like that before and I didn't find it easy.

"When I got back to the surgery the vet had only just returned, but he gave Bess a quick examination and said she might be suffering from a tooth abscess. That would explain why she was not eating and why she snapped every time I went to stroke her head.

"When the vet rang to say he needed to keep Bess in overnight because she'd had an anaesthetic I was beside myself with worry.

"But when I called to collect her I couldn't believe my eyes. She charged at me like a puppy. I know she's lost a bit of weight, but look at her. I'm the happiest man alive."

All the time Ernie was recounting these events he kept gulping down his stout and was soon on to yet another bottle and getting drunker by the minute. His happiness was so infectious if I hadn't had the car outside I might well have joined him in another glass. As I made to leave he doubled up with laughter.

"Those darned foolsh," he slurred. "Overtaking me on such a narrow road, spechially that madman driving the Shierra."

I could see the realisation dawning on his face and quickly made for my car. "Here, rector," he yelled.

"Come to think of it, that Shierra, it looked jusht like yoursh."

It wasn't until I got back to the rectory I noticed Ernie's album still lying on the passenger seat.

Chapter 4

Brambles and Chicken Manure

I should have been the happiest man alive. It was years since we'd had a proper holiday and as a surprise Mary had organised a five-day break. Within a few hours we'd be heading for the coast.

I was dreading it. I'd convinced myself that things would go wrong the moment my back was turned. I slumped back in the chair and stared at my diary. Not a single entry for the week ahead. No Sunday service. No funerals, weddings or christenings. Not even a Church Council meeting. I'd never seen my diary look so empty.

* *

The note I'd hurriedly written was a short one. 'My Dear Mary', it read, 'forgive me, but I must spend some time on my own. I need time to think. I can't go on like this. Always remember I love you'.

Mary was busy packing. I could hear her upstairs, humming along to a tune on the radio, her voice filled with happiness. I should have thrown the note away there and then, but I didn't. Instead I left it propped against a vase of sunflowers in the middle of the kitchen table.

* *

The road I was driving along would take me across the moor towards Brookworthy. I had no idea why I was on that particular stretch of road. Perhaps I was subconsciously heading for Brookworthy Church. I couldn't be sure.

A few yards from a lonely crossroads the sky became a pillow of dark clouds bringing with it layer upon layer of heavy rain. Next minute the car came to a juddering halt and the petrol gauge told me the tank was empty. How could I have been so stupid? Only yesterday Mary had reminded me to fill up ready for our trip to the coast.

In deep despair I cradled my head in my hands and wept. I don't know how long I was there, but when I opened my eyes the dark clouds had passed and the sky was filled with clusters of white clouds, rim-lit as a blazing sun broke through.

I stared at the road ahead and instinctively knew I'd arrived at my own personal crossroads. I must choose which path to take. "Dear God," I prayed. "Dear God, please point me in the right direction." I got out of the car and started walking.

* *

The Fox and Hounds wasn't busy at that time of the day. Jed Gibbings was sitting at the bar and waved me over. "Hello, rector. Bit off the beaten track aren't you? Having a day off?"

I quickly explained how I'd stupidly run out of petrol and hoped someone might be able to help me. In a flash Jed jumped off his stool.

"Tell you what. Let's have a pint together then you come along with me. I can find you a can of petrol."

It was only a short distance to Jed's, and as we ambled along he told me the problems he'd been having. The benevolent farmer, who'd allowed him to park his caravan on wasteland on the edge of one of his fields, had died. It had been a loose arrangement and when the new owners moved in they'd demanded Jed get off their land.

"Only gave me two weeks. Been there for over twenty years, never bothered anyone, and that's how they treated me, saying my caravan was an eyesore and I'd no right to be on their land."

From the outside Jed's caravan looked clean and tidy. He'd painted it cream and green and a metal sign above the door read 'Home Sweet Home'. A row of old chimney pots brimming with flowers added to its charm.

Jed pointed to a wooden bench.

"Take a seat and I'll tell you what happened next." A large tabby cat crawled from beneath the caravan and Jed carefully lifted him on to his lap.

"This is my pal, Sniffer. He's been with me for some fifteen years. Anyway, like I was saying, the new neighbours wanted me off their land, but I knew my rights and I wasn't going anywhere.

"They got so angry they weren't thinking straight and ripped up most of the brambles screening my home. Worse still, those brambles had been home to all kinds of wildlife.

"Next thing, they put up a wire fence. I could feel them watching me. They watched my every move. They even threatened me with the police and as a last resort got the county planning office involved, but none of them wanted to know.

"The feud went on for months. I'm a mild-mannered sort of chap, rector, but now all I could think about was getting revenge."

Jed was smiling to himself. "They tried to drive me out by spreading a load of chicken manure all along my boundary." Jed screwed up his nose. "Phew, the smell and the flies were unbearable. Anyway, I retorted by playing loud music late at night but I don't suppose they even heard it their house being on the other side of the field."

I heard the sound of giggling coming from behind a small clump of brambles. I could just make out two tiny faces peering at me. Were these the neighbours' children, I wondered, come to make more misery for Jed?

"Don't worry, rector. This is Cassie from next door." Jed pointed to the house across the field. "Come here Cassie. You as well, Tom. I'll show you something. Now take a look at this little hole and see if you can work out what sort of animal made it. "

Two children came from behind the brambles and flopped to the ground.

"Can you see any scratch marks, any footprints, any signs of droppings?"

Remembering I was with him Jed said: "You don't know this gentleman, do you? This is Mr Longfield, the rector from Ashenridge."

"So where do you two come from?" I asked.

"We live next door," answered a rather muddy little girl I guessed to be about eight years old.

"And I'm Tom." Tom turned out to be the girl's older brother. "Come and see what Jed found yesterday. He knows everything about the countryside. He's our best friend."

To my amazement they pointed to a fox hole. "Jed says if we're very quiet we might see the foxes come out tonight."

Jed must have read my thoughts and gave me a knowing smile.

"Everything's turned out fine. One bit of good did come out of the wire fence because before I could only hear the kiddies playing far away in their garden. Now I could *see* them. I loved hearing their chatter and their laughter. And Sniffer didn't know any different, did he? He was for ever crawling through a gap in the brambles to go over to them.

"I got to telling them wildlife stories through that fence and they loved it. Cassie and Tom changed everything. I couldn't get anywhere with their parents, but the kiddies brought them round. I could never have done it on my own."

Jed wouldn't take a penny for the petrol. I thanked him and we walked back to the car together, Cassie and Tom running alongside, and poor old Sniffer battling to keep up with us. "Remember what I said, rector, I couldn't have done it on my own."

My spirits rose as I drove back to Ashenridge. Jed's words kept coming back to me – 'I couldn't have done it on my own'. If God had ever spoken to me he spoke to me that day through Jed Gibbings. I thought of his seemingly helpless plight and how, when all else failed,

Cassie and Tom had innocently helped him. Jed's story had brought me to my senses. I was ready to admit that I couldn't cope on my own. The bishop had denied me any extra help and it was down to me to build up a team of lay helpers.

* *

The look on Mary's face when I arrived back at the rectory was a mixture of relief and anxiety. We threw our arms around each other and, still embracing, walked into the kitchen. My wretched note was still where I'd left it, propped against the vase of sunflowers. I snatched it up and threw it into the bin.

How could I have been so selfish? In all these months Mary hadn't complained once and it was thanks to her my diary was empty. She was the one who had spent weeks organising a band of trusted people to take care of the parishes during my absence.

I asked for her forgiveness and, gently kissing me on the lips, she whispered: "There's nothing to forgive, Jack. You've been through a tough time. Things will get better now."

Mary saw me looking at the suitcases. I grabbed one in each hand and made for the door. "What are you waiting for?" I asked. "I thought we were going on holiday."

Chapter 5

Mr Hillyard's Chest

As the months went by the concept of forming a team of
lay helpers was starting to take shape. This was largely
due to Will Swift who, recognising my ever-increasing
work load, was constantly coming up with good ideas.

"Why don't you ask your friend Henry Burrows to
help you? I knew him at agricultural college. He's older
than me, but he went there for a short course as a mature
student. He's told me several times he'd love to help.
Why not take him up on it?"

"Yes," I replied, "I like Henry very much. We're good
friends. He's very Christian in his thinking, and he's also
a person everyone would respect. What a pity he goes to
church so rarely."

"Are you sure that's true?" Will sounded unconvinced.
"At college he was a regular at chapel. In fact it was
Henry who gave me so much encouragement.
Nowadays he goes to the cathedral, more often than you
may think. Why not give him a try. Then there's Sonia
Williams."

"Sonia?" I couldn't hide my surprise.

"Yes. She'd love to get more involved, especially with her husband being the churchwarden at Westaleigh. I know what you're thinking, and you're right, she still prefers all the halleluiahs and clapping at the Pentecostal church in Whiteminster, but she's a fine Christian woman and marvellous when it comes to the youngsters.

"Then there's Mabel Waterhead. I know some people hold her past against her, but given the right job she'd be worth her weight in gold. She has quite a gift you know when it comes to helping the elderly."

Dear Mabel Waterhead! In my early days in Ashenridge she'd gained a reputation for being something of a heavy drinker. I'd never forgotten the afternoon she hurled an empty whisky bottle through our drawing-room window, narrowly missing a prospective curate I happened to be interviewing at the time.

"My, my, Will, you have been busy! Thank you, you've certainly given me a lot to mull over."

Not that long ago I'd stupidly thought God had turned a deaf ear to my prayers. It seemed I was wrong.

* *

Will Swift was not the only one trying to come to my rescue. Brookworthy Church had also taken my troubles to heart and in an effort to reduce my work load they kindly offered to hold their next church council meeting without me.

It was late November and the agenda seemed innocent enough – to sort out the finer details of their Christmas programme. Jonathan Hopkins was due to take the Sunday service, and he offered to attend the meeting afterwards on my behalf.

Things might have gone well had it not been for a large wooden chest, an eyesore which stuck out from the wall at the back of the church. This battered old chest had certainly seen better days, and it might well have remained there for many more years had it not been for Jonathan Hopkins.

After the service Mr Axenham, the churchwarden, asked the members of the church council to gather at the back of the church. As Jonathan snuffled and shuffled his way to join them his cassock caught on a rough edge of the chest and a terrible tearing noise could be heard. Knowing nothing of its history, Jonathan gave full vent to his feelings and demanded to know how such an ugly thing came to be there?

Mrs Redler was the first to speak. "'Twas all wrong," she declared. "They never asked the rector. One day they just put 'n there. Should never of done it."

"So *why* did they put it there?" Jonathan demanded. He was trying hard not to lose his temper, but could not prevent himself from snuffling as he spoke.

"Well," continued Mrs Redler, "'twas after old Mr Hillyard died. They 'ad this old chest. Nobody wanted it when they cleared out 'is workshop so they puts it in church."

"No, no it wasn't like that at all," Mrs Holman chipped in. "You know full well there was nowhere to keep the old hymn books and flower pots. They used to get dumped in the back pew. They looked terrible there so Mrs Hillyard gave the chest to the church. She said it would come in handy for storing things."

Mrs Redler was determined to have the last word. "Pity they said nothing 'til after they'd put it there. A bit of a shock for the rector. Trouble was 'e was too meek and mild. 'Twas an ugly thing then, 'tis an ugly thing now. I reckon 'twas just a way of getting' rid of it."

All talk of Christmas was soon forgotten and a verbal battle broke out. Poor Mr Axenham found it impossible to keep order and in the end it was agreed to call another meeting at which, of course, the rector would have to be present.

* *

I was determined to get my facts right so the day before the meeting I drove over to Brookworthy to take a look at the chest. I bumped into Ted Brannam outside the church.

"If that chest goes, you'll not see me in church again, nor any of my family," he declared. "After all the good Mr Hillyard did for this village, and you want to get rid of it. It's nothing but a disgrace," he snorted in disgust.

This was rich coming from Ted Brannam. The last time I'd seen him in church was at Mr Hillyard's funeral, and that had been several years ago.

The more I looked at the chest the more I realised it was definitely past its sell-by date. It smelt mouldy and the bottom was so rotten it had started falling apart. Damp had swollen the lid making it impossible to shut properly. Inside it was full of musty old hymn books and unwashed jam jars. It would have to go.

I made a point of being there on Mrs Holman's cleaning day. When she saw me bending over the chest she grabbed the opportunity to tackle me about another old chestnut of hers.

For years the church cleaners had been complaining about bat droppings. Not one of them had ever seen the creatures in flight, yet they insisted they had evidence. The issue had often come up at church council meetings, but nothing had been done because most of us knew that the local bat lovers considered their 'flittermice' totally untouchable. They would have created an almighty fuss had we tried to get rid of them.

"We've had bat droppings all over the place. They've even been eating a book someone left at the back of the church. You've got to do something about it."

"Bats in the winter? Bats eating books?"

"Well, I've been told they do come out in the winter, sometimes anyway."

"But eating books?"

This was not the right time to get involved on the subject of bats. I was there to deal with the problem of the chest. I asked Mrs Holman if she'd mind taking a look with me. After all, she would be at tomorrow's meeting. I pointed to some bits of chewed-up paper on the flagstones. Then I carefully pulled up the ill-fitting lid of the chest. Sure enough, deep down I found more pieces of paper which were apparently part of a mouse nest. I showed it to Mrs Holman who screamed in fright and made for the door. I continued taking things out of the chest until I reached the bottom. As I thought, the wood there was completely rotten.

By now Mrs Holman had been persuaded to come back and she inspected my finished work. Looking at the mess I'd exposed she declared: "Rector, you'll have to call in the health inspector. They had a right fuss up at Ashenridge primary when they found mice droppings in one of the classrooms. Said it was a serious health hazard."

How odd, I thought, about mice and their droppings being dangerous. 'Flittermice' droppings didn't seem to count!

* *

"Funny thing where those mice came from," said Mr Axenham when he rang me to say the meeting had been cancelled. "Nobody wants to keep that rotten old chest in the church, and now Mrs Hillyard, bless her, has offered to pay for a smart new cupboard where we can store everything. It'll be in memory of her husband. Still, I can't help thinking it really is a funny thing about those mice. There was no sign of them the last time I looked in that chest. Perhaps I didn't reach down far enough."

"Funny thing," I agreed.

Chapter 6

Parting is Hell

One morning I woke up with a strange feeling that all was not well at Laburnum Lodge. Was it from God? Or was it my imagination? I told Mary about it. She felt it was better to be safe than sorry and before I knew it she'd gone out. After only a few minutes the kitchen door flew open and she was back again, her face as white as a sheet. She was gasping for breath and for an awful moment I thought she had been taken ill. I jumped up from the kitchen table and went to help her, but grasping my hand she yelled: "Jack, Jack, it's Mrs Batchelor. There's something terribly wrong, I think she's…"

Laburnum Lodge is but a few hundred yards from the rectory yet it seemed to take forever getting there. I prayed that Mary was mistaken, but I knew, even before my hand touched her cold forehead, that Mrs Batchelor was indeed dead.

Mary stayed with her while I went into the house and rang for an ambulance. Through the drawing-room window I could see her bending over Mrs Batchelor, holding that dear lady's already cold hands. As I reached the rose garden Mary looked up at me. "Look, Jack, over there." An exquisite hat was dangling incongruously from one of the rose bushes. "She only bought it last week. She loved showing it off to me. And to think we should have been having coffee together later this morning. I can't believe this is happening, Jack."

We watched in silence as they gently lifted Mrs Batchelor on to a stretcher and into the ambulance. We drove behind it to Whiteminster General and gave the staff there as much information as we could, then sat together in an otherwise empty corridor drinking endless cups of tea until one of the staff said there was nothing we could do and suggested we go home.

Once back at the rectory numerous telephone calls had to be made. There seemed no end to it and as the light began to fade I decided to take the phone off the hook. Tomorrow was another day and for now all Mary and I wanted to do was curl up in bed and fall asleep in each other's arms. This had been one of the saddest days of our lives.

* *

The post-mortem revealed that Mrs Batchelor had, as we'd guessed, died from a massive stroke. Her doctor assured us it would have been very sudden, she wouldn't have known a thing. We had to believe him.

Her few remaining relatives, two nieces and a nephew, lived in Scotland. In all the years she'd lived in Ashenridge they'd never visited their aunt, but they were quick to visit now and within a week Laburnum Lodge had been stripped bare.

For her funeral Ashenridge Church was festooned with the most beautiful of flowers and the coffin was adorned with deep-red roses from her beloved garden.

While there was much sadness in the air, everyone acknowledged that the funeral must be a celebration of Mrs Batchelor's life. I conducted the service and said the opening prayer. We sang rousing hymns, among them her favourite Thine Be the Glory, and then it fell to Mary's cousin, Uncle Tiddly, to read a tribute to his dear friend.

Once the bane of Mary's life, over the years her animosity towards her relative had faded and he was now a regular visitor at the rectory. As youngsters our two children, Paul and Ann, had got used to seeing him rather the worse for wear and had fondly nicknamed him Uncle Tiddly, a name that had firmly stuck.

I knew he was nervous and thought that a little Dutch courage would not have gone amiss, but not a bit of it. His voice was strong and he spoke from the heart, not once referring to any notes. He talked about the times he and Mrs Batchelor had spent rambling round the leafy lanes of the Badger Valley, about their regular visits to

National Trust properties, when Mrs Batchelor would return home full of exciting ideas for the garden at Laburnum Lodge. He spoke of her kind and generous nature, and told a very amusing story about the time she unwittingly placed a bird bath on someone's grave. Their friendship had been founded late in life, but it had been a meaningful and a joyful one.

In conclusion, Uncle Tiddly read a poem by one of Mrs Batchelor's favourite writers.

If I should go before the rest of you,
Break not a flower, nor inscribe a stone,
Nor when I'm gone, speak in a Sunday voice,
But be the usual selves that I have known.
Weep if you must,
Parting is hell,
But Life goes on,
So sing as well.

He'd held up until then, but as he recited Joyce Grenfell's moving words his bottom lip started to tremble. He fumbled in his blazer pocket and pulled out a spotted handkerchief, the size of a small tablecloth, and proceeded to blow into it loudly and often. There wasn't a dry eye in the church.

I brought the service to an end with prayers and a blessing and gently reminded the congregation it was

Mrs Batchelor's wish that any donations should go to Ashenridge Parish Church. This was the organist's cue to play the final hymn, Jerusalem, which she did with incredible virtuosity.

We solemnly made our way across the churchyard and laid Mrs Batchelor to rest at the foot of the old stone wall adjoining her very own rose garden.

At the gathering in the parish hall we shared memories about Mrs Batchelor's love of giving surprises, about innocent mistakes made when she forgot to wear her hearing aid and, of course, about her love of picturesque hats. Above all we remembered her numerous acts of kindness and generosity.

Uncle Tiddly sat alone at the far end of the hall. A forlorn figure, he was going to find it harder than most coming to terms with Mrs Batchelor's death. Mary put a comforting arm around his shoulder. "Come on, Will, remember the words you spoke in church only a few minutes ago: 'But life goes on, so sing as well'."

Uncle Tiddly gave a weak smile and straightened his shoulders. "You're right m'dear. Give me a few days. I'll soon pull myself together."

"Why don't you come and spend them with us? You know you're always welcome at the rectory."

Uncle Tiddly's look of relief and gratitude said it all and once again his spotted handkerchief was put to good use.

Over the years Mrs Batchelor had given me plenty of surprises. Always well intentioned, they often landed me in hot water, but with her advancing years the surprises had become less frequent.

Yet she did have a final surprise, and this one was for all of us. It came in the form of a hand-written letter, sent to me by her solicitor, which read:

'To Whom It May Concern. It has been a pleasure and a privilege to be part of Ashenridge. On my death I bequeath the enclosed sum of money to Ashenridge Church in the sincere hope it will provide floral decorations therein for many years to come. Thank you for giving me some of the happiest years of my life. Rosamund Batchelor'.

Her generosity was such that Mary and I sat staring at the cheque in stunned silence. She may not have intended it as a surprise, but that's exactly what it felt like.

I squeezed Mary's hand, closed my eyes, and offered up a silent prayer.

"Goodbye, Mrs Batchelor, and God Bless you. And thank you, Lord, for letting us be the ones to find her."

Chapter 7

Tidd'n No Good

I'd seen him several times, the man with the rosy cheeks, wearing a green woollen hat pulled down over his ears. He never smiled and his face had begun to haunt me.

I'd seen him in a rusty old van driving down one of Ashenridge's remote lanes. On another day I caught sight of him as he emerged from some farm buildings. The next time I saw him was on market day in Leighford and by now we were at the nodding stage. But who was he and where did he live?

Weeks later I saw him boarding the village bus. As I passed by he gave an unsmiling nod through the window. Yet his identity still remained a mystery.

* *

Wesley Peterson, the very aptly named local Methodist minister, was aware I'd been going through a tough time, feeling exhausted and not coping with my workload.

I'd always got on well with the succession of ministers from Leighford, who in turn looked after the little chapel in Ashenridge. From time to time we held joint services and Wesley was wondering if we could help each other even more by sharing visits to parishioners in distant hospitals. Leighford Cottage Hospital was no problem, but anyone needing surgery would go to Whiteminster General, an hour's drive away. More specialist cases might go to regional hospitals, even as far as Bristol, which could take up most of the day.

I jumped at Wesley's idea, but then hesitated. It would only work where our pastoral areas coincided. His Methodists were thinly spread over a much wider area than my parishes.

Wesley took my point and came up with another idea. He had a student, Mel, staying with him, a young man sent out on placement to get some experience working on the rural Methodist circuit. "Let's get him to plan the next joint service in Ashenridge Church. That will take some of the pressure off you. He can be a bit intense, but I'm happy to give his ideas a chance if you are.

"By the way, Jack," he added, "I've been meaning to tell you about Zachary Zeale. Perhaps you've come across him. He's a lonely widower, recently moved into one of the cottages along from the Coach and Horses. You can't miss him, he's got such a rosy face, and rain or shine he wears the same grubby hat. His wife knitted it for him years ago and he can't bear to be parted from it. Wouldn't surprise me if he wears it in bed! Anyway, I think he could do with a bit of help. I must confess I can't get anywhere with him."

So Zachary Zeale was my mystery man, and three days later I happened to come across him in Radd's as he was collecting his pension. I grabbed the chance to make his acquaintance and asked if he liked living in Ashenridge.

"Early days, rector," Zachary replied, shuffling his feet as though unsure of what to say next. "I'm a Methodist, you know, only tidd'n no good. Mr Peterson up to Ashenridge Chapel doesn't understand. He knows nothing about the countryside. Only they say you'm country so I reckon you'd know more than him."

We strolled back to his cottage and he invited me in. It looked sad and uncared for and his few bits of furniture had seen better days. I couldn't help noticing the dishes piled up in the kitchen sink. At least Zachary was feeding himself.

"I tried Leighford Chapel you know. But tidd'n no good. Nobody understood me."

No matter what I suggested his face remained expressionless and I always got the same reply. If I'd told Zachary he'd won a million pounds I felt sure he'd still have said 'tidd'n no good'.

It was only as I turned to leave I noticed a bowl of apples sitting on the windowsill. It must have held three or four varieties and, unlike his furniture, each one looked as though it had been well and truly polished.

"Help yourself, rector. They came from the little orchard out the back there."

I peered through the window and, sure enough, there were two neat rows of apple trees.

"Had a bigger orchard than that where I came from, but that's big enough for me, now I'm getting on a bit."

Zachary disappeared into another room and came back holding a dog-eared book. I could tell by the way he held it against his chest it was precious. He carefully handed it to me. The jacket was torn in places and held together with bits of tape, but the lettering, although a little faded, was easy to read, *The Apples of England* by H V Taylor.

"That book's been in our family for years. Never needed another one. When it comes to apples that's my bible." Zachary gave an embarrassed cough. "Sorry rector, but you know what I mean."

Zachary was at once transported into a world of Orange Pippins, Worcester Pearmains, Upton Pynes and Tidicombe Seedlings and his expressionless face suddenly became animated.

"Me and the missus, we loved them all. Couldn't grow them all mark you, but knew just about everything there was to know about them."

He paused to catch his breath. "Ever heard of Devonshire Quarrendens, rector? Good growers in the West Country. They were our favourites."

I suggested he might like to take a look at the apple trees in our garden. He readily agreed, but before I'd reached the end of the path Zachary had one more question for me. "What do you know about Tom Putt, rector?"

I had to admit I'd never heard of Tom Putt. Zachary smiled. "It's another favourite of mine, and I mention it 'cause that apple got its name from someone like you."

Zachary could see the puzzled look on my face. "Got its name from the Reverend Tom Putt. Thought you might have known that one."

Zachary had been speaking for several minutes without one 'tidd'n no good' passing his lips!

* *

Zachary stood in the rectory garden shaking his head in despair. He was back to his old self. "Tidd'n no good. Your apple trees are in a sorry state. Same everywhere you go round here."

I had to agree with him. Mary and I were so short of time these days we rarely got into the garden except to keep the grass mown and the weeds under control. But Zachary's despondency gave me an idea. True to his word, my dear friend, Henry Burrows, had been attending services at Ashenridge Church. I knew Henry and his wife took a lot of pride in their orchard and

Zachary might well enjoy spending some time there. A few days later Henry reported back.

"I see what you mean about poor old Zachary. I tried to persuade him to give me some advice but, as you know, we only grow common varieties like Blenheims and Bramleys and he wasn't interested. All he did was shake his head and kept repeating 'tidd'n no good'.

"We did get into a discussion though about churches and chapels and he told me about the lively hymns he used to sing as a child but, of course," and here Henry mimicked Zachary, "'tidd'n no good, they don't sing ones like that these days'."

* *

The rectory doorbell rang. A serious-looking young man stood before me. He wore horn-rimmed glasses, a college blazer and a neatly-knotted tie. His voice was incredibly precise.

"Good morning, Mr Longfield, my name is Mel. I believe Mr Peterson said you would be expecting me."

I invited him into the drawing-room and offered him a cup of tea.

"Thank you, Mr Longfield, that is very kind, but I rarely drink between meals. Do you think we could get straight to the point. Mr Peterson has discussed with me the benefits of churches and chapels coming together and I know how you feel about it. I am the same. I feel like beating my breast. If only we could spend more time repenting the wicked divisions between our churches perhaps then we could face the world again. That is why I am so inspired by your idea. I want to bring Ashenridge Church and Ashenridge Chapel together with a service of repentance."

Mel had warmed to his subject and wanted me to look at the document he grasped in his hand.

"It is similar to the one we used at college. It is called a Service of Repentance and Unity."

Mel placed the document in my hand. He gazed at me excitedly and awaited my response. The words 'we repent' appeared in heavy capitals on every page. Then I saw something about 'ashes'. Did he want everyone in Ashenridge to cover themselves in ashes?

While I was searching for the right words he continued. "We are all Judases with our expensive church buildings. I long for the day when half of them are shut and the money given to the poor."

"Mel, actions speak louder than words. If you really want to help I think you'll have to bring things down to our level. We need to prove to the world that churches can work well together. That's what Mr Peterson and I are trying to do.

"Just now there's someone we are both trying to help, and I think it would be good if you called on him. He's a

Methodist, although I don't think he's at all bothered about attending any particular church. He's desperately lonely and needs a sympathetic Christian soul to talk to. His name is Zachary Zeale. Come back to me when you've seen him and let me know how you get on. Then we'll talk some more about a joint service."

I sincerely hoped a visit to one or two people like Zachary would bring Mel down to earth.

I rang Wesley Peterson and we talked about Mel's visit. "I'm all in favour of working together, so are most people round here. I'm sad about the divisions of the past, but I find it very difficult to repent over someone else's sins, especially those who have long since been dead. If I don't find it easy I'm sure others round here won't either. It's like resurrecting yesterday's battles. Mel's idea of a special form of joint service might be a good one, but he might have to be prepared to make some drastic alterations to it." Wesley agreed.

Mel hadn't lost any time and later that day he reported back to me. His voice sounded so earnest. "It is our fault. We have let poor Zachary down. He says God never answers his prayers, but I know what is ruining his prayers, it is because our churches are so divided."

When I told Will Swift what had happened he smiled. "If bright, rousing hymns are the sort Zachary likes then Sonia Williams over at Westaleigh's the one to call on him. She'll cheer him up!"

"What a good mix of helpers we've got," I commented to Will. "Sonia with her rousing singing and tambourines, you and me with our straight Anglican ways, Henry with his love of cathedral music, even Mel. And let's not forget Mabel Waterhead. If we can work together one day we will achieve church unity. What's more, I believe God is somewhere behind all of this. Let's go for Mel's idea of a joint service and let's make more of it than even he imagined."

"You're a braver man than me," Will replied. "On your head be it."

Sonia readily agreed to visit Zachary and I realised the lay team and helpers were at last moving in the right direction.

We were due to meet one evening and I'd been looking forward to it, but the closer it got the more anxious I became. We were all so very different. Could we pull together as a team? Could we make it work? We had to because the future of our churches depended on it.

Sonia started the ball rolling by telling us about her visit to Zachary. It had proved no more successful than any of the others. She found the subject of bright hymns did not last long and the conversation soon dried up. Tears came into her eyes as she recounted how sad and uncared for he and his home looked. She felt she must do something so she offered to pray with him. That was the last straw for poor old Zachary.

Up until then Mel had been happy to sit and listen, confident that we would shortly be approving his ideas. He now stared in horror at Sonia.

"I am sure you meant well, but no wonder poor Zachary reacted as he did. How can we Christians who are so divided amongst ourselves go to someone else's house and *pray*?"

"But that's what we always did at the church I used to go to," Sonia replied. "It's no good sitting around and talking about unity. Action's what's needed."

It was time for Henry Burrows to wade in.

"But we don't want people waving their arms around and clapping. That will scare everyone off. What we need is something quiet and dignified. I know Mel wants to use ashes in his joint service, but could I suggest we use incense instead?"

Henry's words might well have been a try-on, but Mel took them at face value. Pulling his shoulders back and looking directly at Henry over the top of his horn-rimmed glasses he said: "I do not think so, Mr Burrows. Romish incense! Romish incense was hardly what I had in mind."

After an hour of heated discussion I brought the meeting to an end. Mel's proposed service remained untouched on the table, its future uncertain.

The team of lay helpers on which I was setting all my hopes seemed to be heading for disaster. Not for the first time in recent months I wondered if it was time for me to be leaving Ashenridge. Perhaps someone younger, someone with more vision and stamina, should be taking my place.

The following morning Mel called at the rectory. He explained that at college he'd been warned it was unwise and insensitive to march into someone's house and to start praying uninvited. When I pointed out that Sonia had only *offered* to pray he seemed less sure of himself.

He also admitted that Zachary had said something which had stuck in his mind – 'tidd'n no good planting one sort of apple in an orchard, there have to be different varieties'.

As Mel said: "Not so very different to having a choice of churches, is it?"

Later that day Henry Burrows rang and apologised for stirring things up at the meeting. He genuinely believed Mel had to learn that Christian unity did not mean putting everyone into the same straight jacket.

In due course Mel visited every house in the village, but the well-supported united service turned out to be very different from the one he had originally envisaged.

Some folk looked rather uneasy when Sonia introduced a music group from her Pentecostal church who rattled tambourines and clapped their hands rather a lot. It wasn't to everyone's taste when Henry Burrows introduced a friend of his, a choirmaster, who tried to teach us how to sing a piece of plainsong.

Mel's precise manner of emphasising every single word seemed to make ten verses from Luke's Gospel go on for ever. And to top it all, Wesley's solid three-point sermon made everyone late for their Sunday lunch.

But that service did provide us with a better appreciation of the differing styles of different churches.

* *

Mabel, too, was determined not to give up on Zachary. He gradually opened up to her and on one occasion mentioned a favourite story which got him thinking. Mabel in turn recounted it to me.

"It goes something like this, Mr Longfield. I just hope I can remember the way Zachary put it to me."

This is the story of a priest whose house was flooded. When the water got up to the front door, someone shouted to him: "Quick, Father, jump into my boat." The priest replied: "Tidd'n no good, the Lord will rescue me."

The flood reached up to the windowsills. Someone else brought a boat to his window, but the priest still said: "Tidd'n no good, the Lord will rescue me."

The priest had to retreat upstairs, and yet another boat came to his bedroom window. "Tidd'n no good, the Lord will rescue me," he cried.

Eventually he drowned, and when he got to heaven he asked: "Lord, why did you not rescue me?"

The Lord replied: "Well, I did send you three boats, and each time you said "Tidd'n no good."

* *

Zachary now admitted that many 'boats' had tried to rescue him – Wesley, Mel, Sonia, Henry, and others. But in the end it was Mabel Waterhouse who turned his life around. She was the one who persuaded him to go on the annual summer outing, and although he'd been overheard in the post office moaning 'tidd'n no good, it's sure to rain', come the day he was one of the first to get on the coach.

By a simple twist of fate a widow by the name of Dolly Parsons sat next to him on the coach. Not a word was exchanged on the outward journey, but when they arrived at the picnic spot Dolly, who lived in Combe Peter and often went to the church there, offered Zachary a slice of her home-made apple pie. He'd never tasted anything like it. With his passion for apples, and Dolly's love of cooking them, the future was looking rosy in more ways than one.

Some months later Mary and I were heading for the little church at Combe Peter and as we dipped down into the tiny hamlet the gardens on either side of us were at their best. What a wonderful day for a wedding.

Zachary had happily given in to Dolly's wish that the service be held at her church. In return, Dolly agreed to a small reception being held in the tiny school room at the back of Ashenridge Chapel.

We were naturally wondering what had happened to Zachary's woollen hat, and later that afternoon Dolly provided Mary with an explanation.

"I persuaded Zachary to bury it beneath one of the apple trees in the orchard. Seemed only right it should have a proper burial."

Because Zachary was reluctant to give up his orchard, the couple lived in Ashenridge and often attended services at the chapel there. But Dolly still loved the church at Combe Peter and so they spent their time going between the two.

Without knowing it, and without any real effort, Zachary and Dolly had brought Christian unity to their own small part of the world.

Chapter 8

Works of Art

The 'FOR SALE' sign came down and the 'SOLD' sign went up, and in Ashenridge village curiosity reigned. We all wanted to know who would be moving into Laburnum Lodge.

Rumours were spreading like wildfire. Apparently the new owner came from Whiteminster. A tall man, probably in his forties. He was definitely a heavy drinker *and* a womaniser, *and* had ostentatious ideas about replacing Mrs Batchelor's rose garden with a heated swimming pool. It was time I paid him a visit.

* *

This was the first time since Mrs Batchelor's death that I'd visited Laburnum Lodge and I was naturally a little apprehensive.

As he was our nearest neighbour I wanted to make the most of our first meeting. The man standing before me was tall, blonde, and handsome. He wore tight-fitting leather trousers, a bright-red shirt, and his ornate leather cowboy boots had two-inch heels which made him look even taller.

His handshake was firm and he gave a broad smile as he caught sight of my clerical collar. "You must be the preacher. I'm Max, Max Malakhov. Come on in, rector." Max gave me a thoughtful look. "You know, I can't carry on calling you rector, sounds far too formal. If it's okay with you I'll call you Reck. Much more neighbourly."

It came as something of a shock seeing Mrs Batchelor's once-elegant drawing-room turned into an artist's studio. All manner of paintings and sketches were propped against, or hanging from, the walls. An easel stood in one corner, on it a large oil painting of a nude. Max saw me staring at it.

"Like that one do you, Reck?" Max laughed. His deep voice reminded me of someone who drinks whisky and smokes a lot, although I later learnt that neither was true.

"Recognise her, do you?"

I was getting rather hot under the collar and sensed Max was teasing me.

"Yes, actually I do recognise her, Max. Well, that is to say I recognise her face you understand."

It was Betty, the buxom blonde barmaid who worked part-time at the Coach and Horses.

"She comes from round here. She's the model for my art class in Whiteminster."

If first impressions were anything to go by I took to Max. I wasn't too sure about him calling me 'Reck', but walking back to the rectory I decided I actually quite liked it. Mary thought it was hilarious and said she couldn't wait to meet him.

* *

Had it not been for trying to help a distressed widow I would not have found myself in the middle of a crisis that at one point stirred up the whole village. It happened at a time I was encouraging Mabel Waterhead to become more involved in my team of helpers.

The ideal opportunity came when she told me about Mrs Harniford, an elderly lady who had recently been widowed. It had been three weeks since I'd officiated at the cremation of her husband and since then little had been seen of her.

Talking to the sad and lonely was one of Mabel's strengths and I suggested she visit her.

As Mabel approached the house she could clearly see Mrs Harniford's curtains were drawn back and a vase filled with flowers stood on the windowsill. Things looked hopeful. She knocked at the front door and after some fiddling with the lock Mrs Harniford appeared. It was approaching eleven o'clock yet she was still wearing her nightdress.

Through her tears she told Mabel how much she missed her husband, how she was finding it difficult to go out on her own and meet people. She knew it was silly but she had no relatives living nearby. She really needed someone to get her going again. Mabel immediately offered to go with her to the village shop to stock up on provisions.

Somewhat cheered by this, Mrs Harniford went on to talk about her husband and proudly showed Mabel a small painting he'd finished only days before his death. It was no great work of art, but Mr Harniford had obviously put a lot of feeling into it. Some of the things he valued most in life were silhouetted against a vivid blue sky – flowers and vegetables grown in his garden, cricket stumps because, as Mrs Harniford explained, he'd been a keen player in his youth. She pointed to a basket containing several loaves of bread. "My hubbie was a master baker 'til he retired. Made the best bread for miles around here."

As Mabel admired the painting Mrs Harniford said: "Do you know what, since I have no grave to visit I think it would help if I could put his painting in Ashenridge Church, not for ever, just for a bit. I could go to the church, sit there quietly and remember him. Do you think Mr Longfield would mind?"

It would have been churlish to turn down her request and a few days later the painting was displayed on a shelf at the back of the church. That Sunday I was thrilled to see Mrs Harniford in church and at the end of the service I went with her to look at the painting. To our surprise one small painting had now become three. Two postcard-size copies of well-known religious masterpieces had been added to the shelf. Who on earth could have put them there?

* *

It was mid-June and the children at Ashenridge primary had been busy painting pictures of what they'd like to do in their summer holidays. Someone came up with the bright idea of linking the church and the school by inviting them to display their work in Ashenridge Church. A few days later the paintings were pinned to a screen and the Family Service that Sunday was packed with children proudly showing off their work to family and friends. I was drawn to one particular painting which stood out from the rest – a winged figure, wearing a long black dress, floating through a blue sky towards an orange ball.

Seeing me staring at it a little boy started tugging at my cassock.

"Do you know who that is, mister?"

I had to admit I didn't, but I thought it was very good.

"That's you, mister. That's you going to heaven for your holiday!"

Because it had proved so successful, the Church Council now decided to hold a full-blown art exhibition with religion as its theme.

* *

I was surprised to see Max Malakhov coming out of Ashenridge Church, his boots making a tapping sound on the flagstones.

"Hi, Reck. Glad I've bumped into you. Heard about your idea for the art exhibition. Love it. By the way, did you like the small pictures I put on the shelf the other day? Got something much brighter and more modern to show you now. I wanted you to be the first to see it."

As we walked into the church I started to feel uneasy. Max stopped and pointed to a large oil painting fixed to the wall between two stained-glass windows. The painting was of Jesus looking like an inflated balloon. It sent shockwaves through me.

Sensing my reaction, Max quickly explained that he was trying to depict Jesus as King of the world, hence the balloon-shaped body. His work may have been clever and well executed, but my gut reaction was that most people round here would consider it in bad taste.

I had to make Max realise he could not simply stride into a church and put up a permanent fixture. I suspected there was a deeper side to him, and although he didn't attend any of the services, he did seem interested in exploring faith. Max appreciated my concern and, much to my relief, instantly removed his painting.

Word somehow got round that I was encouraging people to use the church as an exhibition centre for religious art. Mathilda Pink brought over a sentimental watercolour of Jesus blessing a group of children. Mr Radd's contribution was rather a grim one of Jonah and the whale. He made it clear he did not want it returned, and who could blame him.

Soon the trickle became a flood. It looked as though everyone in Ashenridge owned a religious painting. It reached crisis point when I found ten particularly ugly ones in worm-eaten frames dumped inside the church porch.

It was time to take action and the Church Council decided to bring forward the date of the official art exhibition on the clear understanding it had to have religion as its theme, and that after the exhibition all the paintings were to be removed.

Because of his knowledge of the art world we invited Max to set up the displays and he jumped at the idea. Later he announced that on the opening day a famous artist friend would add some valuable paintings from his own collection and we agreed to leave a prominent space in front of the altar for them. Things were going well and I had every confidence in Max.

On the day of the exhibition a distraught Will Swift arrived at the rectory urging me to get over to the church before all hell broke loose. By the time I got there a crowd of angry people had gathered demanding that the paintings in front of the altar be removed.

There was no doubting the artist's skill, but it only needed one glance to see why everyone was so incensed. The left-hand panel of his triptych portrayed Jesus being pawed by a sensuous woman and was entitled 'Temptation'. The Crucifixion scene in the middle was surrounded by ruined churches and entitled 'The End'. The right-hand panel depicted the Last Supper where everyone appeared to have had too much to drink. 'Bliss' was its title.

Someone started to laugh.

"You're on to a winner this time, rector. It isn't every day you see this many people in church."

"Thought I'd seen it all on those cheeky postcards at the seaside, but they're nothing compared to this."

"Cor, fancy our rector liking those sort of pictures," said another.

"Don't be daft, rector had nothing to do with it."

"Looks like painting by numbers if you ask me."

And so it went on. A few were thoroughly enjoying the occasion, but most were deeply angry. I needed to defuse the situation.

"Please, please," I appealed. "Whatever you think of the exhibits, at least they've drawn a crowd. I can see a lot of faces here I've never seen before. These paintings are serious works of art and serious art can take some understanding. Look at the one about temptation. Doesn't it say in the Bible that Jesus was tempted? But he didn't give into temptation, did he?"

Some laughed, but there was no mistaking the hostility in Annie Cook's voice.

"Look at the way his mouth is drooling. Thinking is as bad as doing. I call it disgusting. If you think blasphemous things like that," and here Annie pointed her finger at the left hand panel, "are suitable for our church, you'd better find yourself another churchwarden."

"Don't be too hasty, Annie." This was Will Swift. "You must realise Mr Longfield has only just seen these paintings. He had no idea anything like this was going to happen. They've only just arrived courtesy of one of Max's friends."

"Thank you, Will, you're absolutely right."

I was trying to keep my nerve. Walking round the paintings and pausing before each one I continued: "I keep looking at these paintings and I still can't understand them. Is the artist trying to put over a serious point in a provocative way that will make us think? Or is he making fun of the very things we hold sacred? You're a good cross-section of the public and I'd honestly like to hear what you feel about this triptych."

With all the fuss going on I hadn't noticed Len Cooksley sitting in the front pew. "'Tis years ago now, but I went on a trip to Whiteminster Cathedral once. They 'ad a cryptic there. Underground it was."

Mathilda Pink shot Len a condescending look and in a loud voice proclaimed: "If you want my opinion, the artist knows *nothing* about religion. He should be prosecuted. He's nothing but a blasphemer."

"Steady on there," Len exclaimed. "Carry on like that and 'e'll be 'avin' you for decimation of character."

Just then Jim Stillman spoke up. "I'm like the rector. I can't be sure what the artist is trying to say. I don't go to church, but I have great respect for those who do. And I still like looking inside churches. It's where I expect to find a very special atmosphere, of reverence and peace.

"Where the church is doing its job, this attitude influences the whole community. I think these paintings make a mockery of that. If there is a place for them it's not in church. I think they should be removed."

Jim was surrounded by a group of people nodding their heads in agreement. Some began leaving the church muttering that they would only return to look at the other exhibits if the offensive ones were removed.

Will and I quickly dismantled the triptych and locked it away in the vestry. I knew I'd be in for it when Max discovered what we'd done.

In the event I was spared having to call on Max because when I returned home Mary informed me he was waiting in my study.

"Do you realise what you've done? Those brilliant, those valuable paintings have already won awards throughout Europe and America. They've been exhibited in all the top galleries, received accolades from reviewers all over the world. It took me a lot of time and trouble persuading my friend to have them exhibited here. And look how you've treated them. I went out of my way to do something for the church and this is how you thank me."

With that a very angry Max marched back to Laburnum Lodge. How sad, I thought, that what had started out as a sincere attempt to help a distressed widow had come to this.

* *

Later that ill-fated day Max returned to the rectory and before I had chance to say anything he caught hold of my arm. "No, please don't say anything for a moment."

I wondered what on earth was coming next. For a minute or two Max paced round the drawing-room, struggling to put his feelings into words.

"When I first saw those pictures, I feared something like this would happen. It's not that I don't regard them as great works of art, I do. They're exceptional. They almost need to offend, to make people think, but I realise now that showing them at an international exhibition is quite different from a country church. After I'd positioned the triptych I stood out of sight at the back of the church and I overheard the reaction of the first visitors. I should have remembered the artist is an ardent atheist. I'm sorry, truly sorry, for getting it so wrong."

"We all make mistakes, Max. I suspect that once word gets round that the triptych has been removed people will want to come back to take a look at the rest of the exhibits. I noticed some of your paintings in there, and Mary has exhibited two of her watercolours."

"Thanks, Jack." Max paused. "Do you mind if I call you Jack?" I nodded, and warming to me he continued: "You see there's something in my past I can never forget. My father escaped from Russia a year or two after the Revolution. He was not a religious man, but he saw the horror of what happened when the peasants lost all respect for God, for the church, and for anyone they mistakenly identified with their old rulers. Far from the expected joy and freedom, we all know what the

Revolution brought. Some of my relatives were shopkeepers, not well off, yet even so they tried to use the little they had to help the poor. Sadly, in the mad frenzy of the time they were brutally attacked, some were massacred, others sent to labour camps and never heard of again."

Max gave a faint smile. "That's why I like living here. You've got yourself a happy, healthy community. Almost everyone has respect for you, for your church, and for each other. I don't want to spoil that. That was never my intention. I may not go to church, but I firmly believe that respect begins with God and everything else follows. Maybe that's why I believe so passionately in freedom of expression."

Much moved by his words, I asked Max if he'd stay and have a drink with me. After the traumas of the day I certainly needed one.

"Thanks, but no thanks. I never touch the stuff. I'll have a fruit juice though, if you've got one."

We joined Mary in the kitchen and she invited Max to stay for supper. Inevitably we got on to the subject of art again and Max told us he was in the middle of painting a series of watercolours to be exhibited at a London gallery. Imagine our delight when he told us the subject – the rose garden at Laburnum Lodge.

Chapter 9

Call That Giving?

One day I came across a most disagreeable looking man staring at the annual balance sheet displayed, according to tradition, in Ashenridge church porch. He sported a toothbrush moustache and carried a walking stick.

Ignoring my greeting, he looked me up and down and after quite a pause informed me his name was Bates, a school teacher and district councillor from the nearby market town of Leighford.

He addressed me in a most aggressive manner. "I've been studying your church accounts. I see you raised £1,500 last year, and where did it go?" He pointed to the notice board. "To the diocese, to new hymn books, bell ropes, an altar frontal, bookshelves, and have I got this right, *flower vases?* When half the world is starving and millions are without homes you choose to spend your money on *flower vases.* You preach about loving your neighbour. I can't see much evidence of that here."

Before I had a chance to speak Peter Eastridge turned up, still in his working clothes, his muddy boots depositing piles of muck in the church porch.

"Sorry, rector, but I left me glasses 'ere last night. Only I'm a bit dirty like. They'm only just inside. Would you mind?"

In fact Peter's glasses were not 'just inside'. I remembered he'd put them down in the vestry after checking over the collection. This meant I had to collect the vestry key from its hidden place, open up, and retrieve the glasses. I could hardly refuse, yet I had a sneaking suspicion Mr Bates would start attacking Peter the moment my back was turned.

I was right. As I approached the porch I could hear his voice growing angrier and louder. "You call *that* giving? What about the real world outside?"

Peter's face was turning a beetroot colour. I feared he would give vent to his feelings at any moment, but quite uncharacteristically he simply said: "If you wants my advice, listen to the rector. We 'aven't time to throw money all over the place. We 'ave to raise every penny we can to 'old on to our church, this building that's been standin' 'ere long before you and me was born."

With that Peter thanked me for his glasses and, depositing another pile of mud in the porch, turned to leave.

I could barely make out his parting shot and prayed Mr Bates didn't hear it. "If you don't mind, rector, I think it'd be best if I leave you to deal with 'err 'itler."

Mr Bates turned on me again: "You go into your pulpit and preach about loving God and giving to the poor. I tell you, I'm disgusted."

Next, he pointed angrily at another notice appealing for money towards the church organ fund.

I couldn't take much more of this and was finding it hard to stay calm.

"If you'd only listen I'll tell you exactly what this church does for needy people."

Ignoring me again, Mr Bates looked across to the rectory and snorted. "Big building like that, must take a lot of upkeep, and upkeep means money."

This was a bit rich coming from someone who, I later discovered, shared a luxurious house with his wife in a choice part of Leighford.

For many years ours had been a wonderful family home. That was until our son, Paul, left England to live in Africa and our daughter, Ann, went off to do teacher training and then got married and had a family of her own. Nowadays family visits only occurred three or four times a year, especially since Ann had married my curate, Harry Browne who, like me, had to cover several parishes leaving him little free time. But the rectory continued to be the centre of the community with numerous events taking place there. I wondered whether Mr & Mrs Bates would ever have been prepared to share their home in a similar fashion.

Mr Bates was gazing at an old Children's Society poster. Here was my chance. "There's a good example. Only the other day some of our church members raised £50 at a coffee morning for that cause. Money raised like that doesn't always go through the church accounts. Individuals often send it direct to the charity concerned."

"I bet they don't. Not when there are really urgent things like organs to restore. I can see through the lot of you."

Without thinking I said: "Forgive me, but you really are getting hold of the wrong end of the stick."

This was too much for Mr Bates. He gave me a withering look, waved his walking stick in the air and snarled: "That does it. Now you're poking fun at me."

I attempted to calm the situation. "I suppose it's the same with schools. Their managers have a responsibility to raise funds and attract grants to keep their buildings in good order. We would soon know about it if classrooms became sub-standard. But schools, just like churches, encourage people to help the needy. In both cases they keep different accounts to cover different aspects of their work. Surely you're not suggesting we should give all of our money to the needy and let school buildings as well as churches go to rack and ruin?"

Mr Bates was in no mood to listen and giving a final grunt he marched off down the church path, venting his rage by stabbing at the gravel path with his walking stick.

Later that morning I fulfilled a long-standing promise and looked in on the Ladybirds who met one morning each week to knit clothes and toys for good causes. What I saw that day was a real eye opener.

Mrs Pearse was well into her eighties. For many years she'd run the Mothers' Union but had eventually handed that job over to a younger woman. She could easily have sat back thinking her duty to society had been accomplished. Instead she organised the Ladybirds, whose hand-knitted clothes and toys were sent to a village in Africa.

I found a dozen elderly ladies packed into her tiny living room, their noisy chatter and clicking knitting needles making quite a racket, but it was a happy sound. Although most of these ladies went to church or chapel, they did not want to be known as a religious organisation and anyone was welcome to go along and join in. They had one golden rule - no gossiping.

They might not call it gossiping, but they all knew what was going on in the village and that morning their main topic of conversation was the 'home for the homeless' somebody wanted to set up in Ashenridge.

Mrs Pearse, in her unquestioning way, thought it was a wonderful idea. She talked about clothes they could knit for the less fortunate, and she remembered pictures of the waifs and strays Dr Barnardo had rescued from the slums of London a hundred years before.

Some of the ladies were not too sure about all of this, but Mrs Pearse was so kind-hearted nobody wanted to disagree with her. I stayed for a cup of tea and, having congratulated them on their wonderful work, left them to carry on with their knitting.

I wondered if there was any truth in what they'd said about the home for the homeless. I did not have to wait long to find out.

At lunchtime Peter Eastridge rang to warn me that a storm was brewing in the parish. Several months ago Steven and Sylvia Watson had decided that Ashenridge House was too big for them. They'd sold it to a young couple who were seeking permission to turn it into a refuge for broken families.

Peter had replaced Steven as Chairman of the Parish Council and feared the proposed change of use would cause quite a stir in the local community. He wanted to know what I thought about it.

I asked Peter to give me a chance to find out a little more. I had in fact met the couple concerned only recently. They came from the Midlands and I'd been introduced to them at a social event in my role as rural dean.

I contacted them and they told me their plan – to provide short-term care and counselling for those whose marriages had broken up. Sometimes a separated couple could be brought back together. In other cases it was a question of housing one of them for a few weeks until new accommodation could be found. They believed that, given the opportunity, stressed folk could benefit from spending some time in the quiet of the countryside. Away from their familiar surroundings they might be able to sort out their problems.

It sounded like a good idea to me, and no serious threat to anyone, so I told them I would do my best to support their application.

This did not take into account the rumours that were spreading round the parish, as I discovered when I popped into the Coach and Horses that evening.

"Dirty foreigners. They'll ruin the place."

"Will be the end of the school, wrecked by rowdy kids."

"It'll be hell here at night with drunks all over the place."

"So what do you think, rector?" Jim Stillman asked me, stroking his chin.

"Well, I never judge something until I know all the facts. That's why I made a point of meeting the couple concerned."

There were murmurs of approval all round, everyone anticipating that since I knew the facts I'd be in a position to write off the whole thing.

I tried to reassure them that the couple intending to run the home were sound people and that stays there would be very brief with only a dozen or so being accommodated at any one time. This wasn't what they wanted to hear.

"Give 'em an inch, and they'll take a yard with the church and the council all behind 'em."

"I know what they'm like. Start off with a dozen, soon it'll be a 'undred, like they 'vacuees."

"'Twas like that in a village near Badgermouth. Said they were going to allow half a dozen caravans for the homeless in a field. Now the whole place is covered in them."

My name was mud. I was seen as a gullible old fool being taken in by do-gooders.

I was not surprised when only a handful of loyal worshippers attended church the following Sunday.

* *

Unknown to me, about a week later two complete strangers fell into conversation while in the doctor's waiting room in Leighford. One was Max of Laburnum Lodge, the other Mr Bates.

On discovering that Max lived at Ashenridge, and also that he was the closest neighbour to Ashenridge Church, Mr Bates held forth about the iniquities of the village and its church. My name cropped up and Max was quick to inform him I was the person who had spoken in support of the proposed home for broken families.

Mr Bates looked surprised. "That's news to me. I'm on the district council. I'll make sure it gets approval."

"Yes," replied Max. "I suppose it will make quite a difference to the village, mothers coming here with problem teenagers. I imagine you'll have to make special arrangements for them at your school."

Mr Bates fell silent as he took in the implication of Max's remark.

A few days later Max contacted Mr Bates saying he strongly agreed that Ashenridge needed to be shamed into further action. In fact he was pretty sure the rector was already thinking of appealing for toys and clothes for families in need. Since Mr Bates and the council cared so much about deserving people all he need do was arrange for the gifts to be collected from the church and distributed where most needed.

Max was not entirely surprised when Mr Bates seemed a little reluctant to do this. In fact he got the distinct impression he'd modified his views about Ashenridge. Was this simply because he was a very busy councillor and teacher, or was he worried about the potential impact a succession of problem children might have on his school?

* *

I was away on a three-day conference and had no knowledge of a letter which appeared in that week's *Leighford Echo* headed 'A Charitable Village'.

I hear the people of Ashenridge are up in arms because someone has applied to open a refuge for broken families in their village. I've been told on good authority that most of the money they raise is spent on the church. Since they never give anything to the less fortunate, clearly it is high time they did something to help needy families. In view of their selfishness I hope the authorities will disregard the objections of the villagers and approve the proposed application. (Name and address supplied).

* *

When I returned home Mary showed me the newspaper. Who could have written such a letter? Concerned and uncertain as to how to handle matters, I went over to the church to pray. By the main door I was surprised to find half a dozen plastic bags. Four contained children's clothes, the others a sad mixture of second-hand toys.

I could hear the familiar sound of Max Malakhov's boots as he entered the church.

"Good evening, Jack. Thought I saw you. They tell me it's all your fault the church is filling up with second-hand clothes and toys."

I didn't understand and asked Max for an explanation.

"You see, you've put us all to shame. What you said the other day in the pub, about the refuge, that was pretty brave stuff. It may not have gone down very well at the time, but it made people think. It seems you were not alone in your views. Someone wrote a letter to the paper. Now everyone's keen to collect for the homeless. That's what all these bags are about."

"But, Max, this simply does not add up. I'm in bad odour with most folk round here because they think I'll be responsible for flooding the place with drug addicts and sex maniacs. Someone writes a letter to the press condemning the village, and a few days later the church is filled with gifts for the homeless. It simply doesn't make sense."

Max gave me a knowing look. "I can't think how people got that impression, but there's an idea going round that if the village gives generously to the homeless we won't be expected to have a refuge on our doorstep. It's odd where these ideas come from, but you know what people are like."

Not another word was spoken, but I knew without a shadow of a doubt that Max was the perpetrator of the letter in the *Leighford Echo*.

* *

As the day drew near for the council to consider the application for the refuge an uneasy truce settled over the village. In the event the crowd who turned up for the meeting were disappointed. Instead of presenting detailed plans, the district council had sent a note saying that the proposals had been withdrawn. Apparently the couple concerned could not afford to carry out the numerous alterations the council demanded of them.

The letter was signed by none other than District Councillor Harold Bates.

That, however, was not quite the end of the story. For weeks the plastic bags remained piled up at the back of the church. They were becoming a nuisance and still growing in number. I contacted Max who promised to have them removed.

Mary was in church the following Friday arranging flowers. To her amazement several boys from Leighford School came crashing through the door. Their teacher, whom the boys called Mr Bates, constantly waved his walking stick at them and in a loud voice issued instructions that they get a move on and load the bags into the minibus.

Mary enquired where the bags were being taken. Mr Bates replied, in a somewhat off-hand manner, that it really wasn't anyone else's business, but as far as he knew they were going to social services.

One of the last boys to leave the church accidentally bumped into Mary.

"Sorry, but sir's in a hurry. We've got to get the minibus back in time to take the school sports team to Whiteminster."

Mary was still curious. "So what happens to all these bags you're collecting?"

"Sorry, I don't really know, but on the way over I think I overheard Mr Bates telling the driver to make sure he took them all to the dump."

Mary couldn't wait to get home and tell me about her brief encounter. She sounded exasperated. "That Mr Bates. I knew I'd seen him somewhere. It was last week, at a coffee morning in Leighford. They were raising money to buy equipment for the school's new sports hall."

I could think of a number of names to describe Mr Bates. Hypocrite was the first one that sprang to mind.

* *

Several weeks later I was in the village shop and heard a lot of panting and puffing coming from the doorway. It was Mrs Pearse and a fellow ladybird struggling with a large parcel. I helped them carry it to the post office counter and couldn't help noticing it was addressed to an African missionary.

Mrs Pearse tipped her handbag upside down and dozens of coins rattled on to the counter. "Sorry about that, Mrs Radd, but there should be enough there to cover the postage."

She gave me a radiant smile. "That's from the Ladybirds. We like to make sure we send our presents to the missionary in good time for Christmas."

"But who's paying for the stamps?" I asked.

"Our menfolk saw to most of that. They cut down on their smoking and drinking during Lent and put the money aside. And the Ladybirds made up the rest with a cake stall. The money soon mounted up."

How I wished Mr Bates had witnessed all of this. How I wished I could have looked him in the eye and said: "Now, Mr Bates. That's what I call giving!"

Chapter 10

Cassocks and Scent

Eric Downing had a habit of saying the clergy were nothing but a bunch of silly old women in long frocks. Unfortunately what he witnessed one day only confirmed his worst suspicions.

Anyone seeing Eric for the first time might think he was a harmless sort of a chap, but in fact he was a self-opinionated individual, and a penny-pinching one at that. I'd had a few tussles with him over the years and knew how he could react if he thought he was being thwarted.

He regarded me with great suspicion. Many years ago I'd supported him when he fell out with most of the parish over his plans to turn one of his farm buildings into a paper-shredding factory. For a while he became almost friendly, but that didn't last.

Eric wanted to retire and was having no luck selling his farm. One of the regulars at the Coach and Horses unwittingly referred to his farm as being 'rather antiquated'. The only potential purchaser at that time, who happened to be having a drink in the pub that very evening, overheard this comment and used it to lever the price down. I'd told Eric time and again it had nothing to do with me, I was an innocent bystander, but he insisted it was my fault and that it had cost him thousands of pounds.

Now in his sixties, Eric was enjoying his retirement and lived with his wife, Dora, in a modern bungalow in Westaleigh. He may not have got top price for his farm at Ashenridge, but he and his wife were considered well off. He should have been content with his lot, but old habits die hard and Eric still went around in worn-out working clothes, and Dora, his long-suffering, down-at-heel wife, was discouraged from buying anything new.

Eric had strong opinions on almost every subject and was not afraid to express them. In his eyes the clergy were nothing but meddlers in other people's affairs, all of them on the make raising funds for church buildings when they ought to be giving to the poor.

He was not easy to live with, and his children left the family home as soon as they could. Then one day his eldest daughter, Mandy, who still lived locally, fell in love with Roy, a charming but rather shy young man from Ashenridge.

Mandy and Roy were keen to have a small church wedding, but knowing of her father's poor opinion of the clergy, and well aware that neither of them could stand up to him, they went ahead and made all the arrangements, only telling Eric when matters were settled.

"You'll find Eric Downing will want to run the whole show," Will Swift warned me. "He'll expect his own way over everything. It was he who demanded they have the wedding at Ashenridge. He reckoned the little church at Westaleigh wasn't important enough."

"But he said he wanted to see me over some small detail," I protested. "I think it was something to do with the photographer."

Will was adamant. "If Eric's involved you can be sure he'll stick his oar in somewhere. And you know he's got an awful bee in his bonnet about the clergy."

* *

My diary for the week ahead was chock-a-block with appointments and so I rang Eric and suggested we meet the following week.

"Why not today?" he demanded.

I tried to make it clear I couldn't drop everything.

"Can't you leave your rectory for a few minutes and do something useful. And while I think of it, I'd prefer you didn't come here wearing one of your frocks."

I ignored his rudeness. I was well aware of Eric's views about clergymen and their cassocks. Whilst it was the custom of some Anglican clergy to wear one at all times, it had never been my habit to wear robes when out visiting.

Within minutes of putting the phone down Mr Oswald, the undertaker, was on the line. An old lady who'd once lived in Westaleigh had passed away. Her family wanted the service to be held in Westaleigh Church followed by a cremation. Mr Oswald was having difficulty fixing a time at a very busy Whiteminster Crematorium. They could only offer three o'clock on the very afternoon I was due to visit Eric Downing. I made a quick calculation and decided I could squeeze in both appointments. I was not to know that two members of the family had to travel a long distance and would arrive late. Furthermore, I had made no allowance for driving three of the mourners from the church service to the crematorium then back again to Westaleigh.

Normally I would have changed into ordinary clothes between services, but with time being so short I had no choice but to leave my jacket behind and drive off to the crematorium still wearing my cassock.

My passengers turned out to be three elderly sisters. They looked alike and they dressed alike, even down to carrying the same crocodile-skin handbags. And each of them wore the same perfume. By the time we reached the crematorium my car reeked of lilies of the valley.

The committal at the crematorium, normally a short affair, should have given me plenty of time to change before going to see Eric, but my three passengers ignored my pleas to hurry and spent ages chatting to long-lost friends.

Having dropped the three ladies off at Westaleigh I dashed to the church. The vestry had been locked and I had no way of retrieving my jacket. I would have to stay in my cassock.

Unfortunately, I was some twenty minutes late, and a disapproving Eric was jumping up and down at his gate.

He yanked the car door open and recoiled in horror as I emerged in my 'frock'. As if that wasn't enough, he now picked up the scent of lilies of the valley. And worse was to come because one of my passengers had left her crocodile-skin handbag lying on the front passenger seat. The look of contempt on Eric's face said it all.

It soon became clear that Eric supposed booking the church was rather like hiring a hall. He considered that what happened during the wedding service lay entirely in his hands.

"This won't take long," Eric declared. Here's the service. A ten minute ceremony, one peal of bells at the end, and we're off."

With a look of disdain he handed me a copy of the very brief civil marriage ceremony which he expected me to use. I cleared my throat and tried to find the right words.

"Tell me," I asked, "when you had a sick animal on your farm, what did you do?"

For a moment Eric was taken aback. Looking puzzled, he replied: "Called the vet if I had to, but what's that got to do with you?"

"So, when the vet came to tend a sick animal, did you tell him how to do his job?"

"No, but that's different," he retorted.

"But it isn't. He's the professional. He's asked to do a job, and it's up to him to decide how it's done. It's the same with me and your daughter's wedding service."

I explained that I could only use a form of service lawfully authorised by the church, and that I acted both as minister and registrar. After all, he did want Mandy and Roy to be married properly, didn't he?

There are various options within the service, and Roy and Mandy had already chosen the ones they wanted. In fact they wanted a simple wedding, but that was not good enough for Eric. He insisted on going over the whole thing again.

"We're not having hymns after all," he declared. "And only one peal of bells. I'm the one who'll have to pay." And so it went on with Eric insisting he was the one providing the money so he would have the final say.

Our final tussle came when discussing the wedding photographs. Eric was adamant the cameraman should have complete freedom throughout the service, insisting he be allowed to take close-ups of the couple.

"God knows how much he's going to charge me. I might as well get value for my money."

Nothing I said was right. In the end I had to remind him that I'd officiated at dozens of weddings and I knew exactly what I was talking about. But Eric Downing was in no mood to listen.

* *

Two days before the happy event Mandy and Roy came to the church for the final rehearsal. Thankfully, the bridesmaids and pageboy already knew what they had to do. So did Mandy's mother, who sat alone in the front pew without saying a word.

I remembered Will Swift's words. How right he'd been. Despite Mandy and Roy's wishes, Eric was adamant he would see to everything and I got the distinct feeling they were happy to let him get on with it, even down to the reception in the hall, which he'd hired for 'one hour and not a minute more'.

"No, no, no," he yelled, prancing round the church like a film director. "You stand over there. The camera goes there. Listen to me you idiot."

I had to remind him we were in a church, not a television studio.

A rehearsal which should have taken thirty minutes went on for a good hour, and Eric still wasn't satisfied.

* *

Most weddings are joyful occasions, but I was not looking forward to this one. I had visions of Eric making objections in the middle of the vows. He'd once asked me if our organist played requests should some of the guests prefer to sing different hymns! Thank goodness he'd decided against having any.

The ceremony was due to begin at noon and I had the morning free. As the weather was set fair Mary asked if I could finish painting the veranda surrounding part of the rectory. I changed into some old clothes and had nearly finished the job when I suddenly remembered I hadn't completed the marriage registers which have to be signed as part of the service.

Still in my paint-splattered clothes, I dashed over to the church. I should have known from past experience that you often get one or two guests arriving early for a wedding and as I passed through the lych gate I heard a car drawing up. By the time I'd found the key and grappled with the vestry lock I could hear voices in the church. Unfortunately the vestry had no outside door. I was trapped.

I could hear Eric's voice telling his wife to hurry up and sit in the front pew. He then told Roy and his best man to stand right where they were and not move until the ceremony started.

There was no way I could leave now. Knowing that Eric's interference could ruin the happiest day of their lives, I was determined not to let Mandy and Roy down.

I found a faded old cassock in the vestry which, although torn under the left arm, would at least cover most of my paint-splattered clothes. If I buttoned up my grey shirt and inserted a strip of white cardboard at the top it would just about pass as a clerical collar. The surplice, hanging on a peg behind the vestry door, was far too small for me, but if I squeezed into it at least the tear in my cassock would be covered. This left my hands. There was no way I could get the smears of green paint off them, but luckily a pair of kid gloves had been languishing in 'lost property' for several weeks. They would have to do.

Eric was totally unaware of my presence as I crept up behind him. I gave a short cough and he spun round. If I looked funny he looked even funnier.

His morning suit had to be a hand-me-down from his grandfather, or even his great-grandfather. A white waistcoat, yellowing with age, was coming apart at the seams. In his hand he held an ancient top hat which he repeatedly waved in the air as he issued orders. He was Thomas the Tank Engine's 'Fat Controller' personified.

Rather lamely he explained that the best man and the bridesmaids had forgotten some of the instructions I'd given them. In view of all the fuss he'd made at the rehearsal this did not surprise me

What's more," he added, "my official photographer still needs to be briefed."

"In that case how fortunate I'm here," I said sarcastically. "We've got enough time to go over things once more and get everything right."

"Don't take too long. My Mandy's been sitting outside in the car all this time. No point in hiring a wedding car when I could drive her here myself."

By now the guests had started arriving and Eric turned his attention to them, continually waving his top hat in the air and yelling out instructions.

Despite my misgivings the wedding got off to a reasonably good start. Perhaps because of nerves, but more likely because he thought it would save money, Eric dragged his daughter down the aisle at such a sprint they arrived at the altar in record time, but at least they arrived together, if a little out of breath. The bridesmaids and the pageboy had a hard job keeping up with them.

Roy only had eyes for his future wife, and as she drew alongside him he mouthed the words 'you look beautiful'. In a loving gesture, Mandy now turned to her mother and placed her bridal flowers in her arms. I'll never forget the radiant smile on Dora's face.

The one person I had not reckoned on was the photographer, a pal of Eric's showing off a brand new camera. In his excitement he forgot my instructions about filming from a discreet spot. I could tell by the way people were looking that something odd was going on behind me. It was the photographer, all but brushing my cheek as he captured the moment Mandy and Roy exchanged vows.

"Sorry, mate," he apologised, giving me a roguish grin. A few minutes later he was climbing over the choir stalls. Wherever I looked, whichever way I turned, there he was with his camera at the ready. Enough was enough. I allowed him to take one more shot, and one only, until we came to signing the registers at the end of the service.

Eric was keen to make the most of signing the marriage registers. He produced a magnificent gold fountain pen from his top pocket then paused, pen in hand, ready for action.

"You'll want all my names?"

"No," I said firmly. "Just your usual signature."

Eric made another flourish with his pen. This time it slipped out of his hand, splattered my surplice with black ink and landed on the floor. As I bent to pick it up the left sleeve of my surplice caught on a sharp edge of the table and the two parted company, revealing my shabby cassock and dirty old shirt.

As I returned the pen to Eric he muttered under his breath: "If that's what he wears, no wonder he covers it up with a frock."

This was too good an opportunity for the cameraman, who proceeded to dance around taking several more photographs. For some inexplicable reason he persisted in focussing on my face.

When it came to signing the second register Eric flourished his pen again, at which point everyone gasped and took several paces back anticipating another accident.

The bells rang out as the bridal party departed, and with profound relief I returned to the solitude of the vestry. I caught sight of myself in the mirror only to discover I had carried out a wedding service with my right cheek daubed in green paint.

By the time I had completed the wedding forms and put everything away the church was empty. Everybody was outside now in glorious sunshine where more photographs were being taken. All was silent inside the church and with the coast clear I started to extricate myself from what was left of the surplice. I then removed my cassock. There was a tap on the vestry door and to my dismay Roy stood there, gazing in disbelief at my paint-splattered clothes.

"I don't usually wear clothes like this under my robes, Roy. There is a good reason for it."

"Don't worry, Mr Longfield. All I wanted to say is that when you came up against Eric this morning you handled him magnificently. Mandy and I wanted to tell you how grateful we are for the way you stood up to him.

"I always used to think a wedding service was a bit of an excuse for a party. I know better now. It wasn't only how you miraculously appeared behind Eric at the right moment, and the way you coped with your own difficulties. If God helps us as he helped you, I know Mandy and I will have many years of happiness. Thank you for everything."

I waited until Roy had gone and when I thought the coast was clear made for a small side door which led out of the church. As I stepped outside who should happen to wander by but Eric himself, still smelling strongly of a potent aftershave. Evidently he'd grown bored with all the photography and was taking a short walk. At that moment he had removed his glasses and was polishing them furiously with a handkerchief. Squinting at me in my old clothes he exclaimed: "Well, well. For a moment I thought you were the rector. I didn't realise they were painting the church. You'd better have a word with him – he goes around in a frock, wears scent, and now he's got himself a handbag."

The temptation was too great. "Tell you something, Eric," I chuckled. "I do like your aftershave."

Chapter 11

A Waste of Space

"That'll last," he said contentedly, looking up from his work and addressing his remark to a tree somewhere over my right shoulder. "The council took me down to the quarry to select my own stones. Picked out the best I could."

Then, bending down to choose the next stone, he commented: "Only there's always one that's no good. Look at that one, a real toad."

Rex Webber pointed to a round stone that seemed to have slipped in amongst the neat square ones he was using. I was much impressed by Rex's workmanship, and proud of a council that used traditional methods to maintain its walls.

* *

There is something deeply satisfying about a well-built dry stone wall. A wonderful traditional craft, its builder knows that long after he is gone his work will live on. The walls of some of my churches were built nine hundred years ago and remain as strong today as they were then. Such thoughts passed through my mind as I watched Rex rebuilding a retaining wall a short distance from the rectory. This structure played an important part in holding back a bank of earth and rocks that towered high above a sunken lane. Little did I know the sequence of events that would follow on from Rex's work.

Some months before, heavy rain had brought down part of the original wall. At the time the council had carried out an emergency job to make things safe for anyone passing by. Nevertheless, a trickle of small stones and lumps of earth continued to fall into the lane. Now, much to my relief, it was being rebuilt, and who better fitted for the job than Rex?

Rex was a shy man who had a habit of avoiding direct eye contact by looking over the shoulder of anyone he was addressing. Making conversation with him had never been easy, but it had improved once I got to know him better. I started the conversation by talking about dry stone walling.

"Trouble was they didn't put in enough drains when they first built it," Rex explained. "You see, the storm water just built up behind and in the end it broke through at the weakest point, bringing down a lot of the wall with it. I couldn't simply put back the stones that had come down. I had to start from the bottom, only this time I put in drains."

Rex pointed to a pile of small earthenware drainpipes and then showed me where, at regular intervals, he had fixed these into the wall. Then he bent down and carefully selected the next stone he was going to use.

"That won't come down in a hurry," he assured me as he carefully placed the next stone in place, tapping it home with a well-worn lump of wood.

* *

A fortnight later I happened to pass along the same way. As I got near I could hear pop music. When I rounded the corner I saw a young man, a cigarette drooping from the corner of his mouth, carelessly adding the final layers of stone to Rex's wall. The difference in the quality of workmanship screamed at me. This young man's shoddy work would never stand the test of time.

"Good thing Rex is home this week," the self-assured young man informed me, shouting above the noise of his transistor radio. "He's been working here for three weeks and the council reckoned it would take him the same again. Anyway he's home with flu now, so I've been given the job."

The young man's name was Wayne, an eighteen year old who'd recently completed a week's course on dry stone walling. What was more, he'd been given a certificate as proof of his proficiency, thus making him an 'expert'.

Shouting above the music I thanked him for his information and said I would be interested in seeing his work when it was completed. In view of what happened later perhaps I should have said more at the time, but I'm not sure what difference it would have made to such a self-assured young man.

* *

"Didn't you know about it?" A surprised Will Swift asked me at a staff meeting several months later. "Why, only last week Tim Bristow was very nearly killed. Found unconscious under a pile of stones and rubble when that newly built wall, the one close to your rectory, collapsed on him. You must remember, it was the wall you praised so much when you saw Rex Webber building it. If only they'd let him finish the job, not that he'll be able to do it now. The council have been making redundancies and suggested he take early retirement."

I looked at Will in horror. "I can't believe it. A boy nearly killed and Rex retired, and I knew nothing about it. That's the trouble nowadays. I'm expected to be here, there and everywhere and I don't even know what's going on outside my own front door. If I'm not around when any news breaks everyone takes it for granted and assumes I know about it anyway."

"It's all right," Will reassured me. "I made a point of visiting the Bristows. It seems that Tim and his brother, Peter, were out on their bikes. It was a gusty afternoon and Peter's baseball cap blew off and got caught in a bush above that bit of the new wall. Tim helped him scramble up to get it, but the top part gave way. Peter slid down unharmed, but Tim wasn't so lucky and ended up under a pile of stones and earth. Peter was convinced his brother was dead, but fortunately he'd only been knocked unconscious. He had to stay in hospital overnight and went home the next day with nothing worse than cuts and bruises. He had a lucky escape though. I explained you were away at a rural deans' meeting."

"Thanks for that, Will, but what about Rex?"

"Being in his sixties he was close to retirement anyway, but he still can't believe he'll never be going back to his old job. He spends his days at home now and I would imagine he's pretty bored. I just hope they find someone who really knows how to finish off that wall. The council was furious with Wayne's shoddy work and sacked him."

The very next day I visited Rex and apologised for not knowing about his retirement. Having been a hard worker all his life I wondered how he was coping not having a job. I also wanted to make sure someone was keeping an eye on him, but all I got was a vague 'I'm all right'. The conversation was drying up and in desperation I asked if he would mind making me a cup of tea.

Rex warmed to the idea and became more relaxed. He actually named a couple of people living nearby who were calling on him. He then went on to talk about the wall. To my surprise he seemed sorry to hear that Wayne had lost his job. He thought there was a lot of good in the lad, nothing that a bit of supervision wouldn't have put right.

"A pity the council pensioned me off. I might have been able to help him."

"So how are you using your time now?" I asked.

"Come and see," Rex replied. On a table in the front room stood a model of an ancient Titan tractor. He let me handle it. It was superb, exactly to scale. How incredible, I thought to myself, that Rex's enormous hands, capable of handling such heavy stones, could create models like those before me on such a small scale. Rex glowed with pride as he went into detail about how he'd crafted the tractor and described others he was planning on building. Then he suddenly went very quiet.

"Are you all right, Rex?"

"I am some of the time, but the days drag a bit you know, and I get to wondering what's the point of being here. I'm just a waste of space."

"No Rex, that cannot be true. Why do you feel that way? Has someone said something to you?"

"Not really. I can see it for myself. When Audrey died all those years ago it felt like the end. It might have been different if we'd had kids. But at least I was busy with my work, work I loved, and that's what got me through. Not much point in life now the council have finished with me. It's true, Mr Longfield, I am a waste of space."

As Rex poured the tea I tried to make him understand why he came over to me as a very special kind of person.

"You're a great craftsman, you always set high standards, not just for yourself but anyone working with you, like Wayne for instance. Given the chance you'd soon have put him right. That's how he'd have learnt. Certificates alone mean very little. When the council put a job in your hands everyone knew it would be done properly."

Rex, still looking despondent, poured another cup of tea.

"It's the same with me. I'll give you an example. People who normally swear a lot modify their language when I'm around, and I've been told that when I attend parish council meetings the atmosphere improves because people try to be on their best behaviour. Believe me, Rex, you are not a waste of space. Whether you're building stone walls or making model tractors, everything you do you do well, and you inspire others."

* *

Several months later I had reason to call on Max Malakhov. He was out, but I noticed someone working in his garden at Laburnum Lodge, a man in blue overalls carefully sorting through a pile of honey-coloured stones. Even with his back to me I knew who it was.

"Good morning, Rex," I exclaimed in delight. "Good to see you back on your old job."

Rex started up from his work and, addressing his remarks towards the church tower over my left shoulder, replied: "Thank you, rector. The council didn't want me so now I'm working for Leighford Landscapers. They're always wanting stone walling done somewhere. They pay me by the job which suits me down to the ground."

"I'm delighted for you, Rex."

"And I've got an apprentice working with me now."

Much to my amazement Wayne appeared, whistling happily to himself as he pushed a wheelbarrow full of stones. I gave him a smile and watched as Rex stood to one side and let him select the next stone and fit it neatly into the wall.

"There, Pop, it'll be a fair number of years before that one falls out."

Wayne turned to me. "I'm not sorry I lost my job with the council, in fact I'm glad. Thanks to Rex I'm learning how to build a dry stone wall the traditional way, the proper way. I mustn't stop though. I've still got half a lorry load to wheel over and when that's done we'll be off to the Coach and Horses for a bite of lunch."

As Wayne walked away he called out to Rex: "And don't forget, Pop. We need to sort out the details for next week's darts match while we're there."

"He's a different lad now." Rex looked on fondly as Wayne filled the wheelbarrow with another pile of stones. "It was me who managed to get this job for him."

"So, you're not such a waste of space after all, are you Rex?"

Chapter 12

Chapels and Pints

"U's never 'eard the like of it. They'm turnin' the chapel into some kind o' club now with loud music and discos," announced Bert Bending in the Coach and Horses one lunchtime.

Bert, a large, gipsy-like character with dark bushy eyebrows and a drooping moustache, always delighted in getting a rumour going, probably to divert attention from his own sins.

He drove a thoroughly unroadworthy van that seemed to have more bits missing every time I saw it. One day it was a wing mirror, then the glass from a side window had disappeared. On another occasion someone had retrieved a pair of windscreen wipers from the middle of the road and it was only by sheer luck Bert found them hanging from the notice board in the bus shelter.

That very morning I'd noticed the rear number plate, which Bert had attempted to tie on with binder twine, had come loose and was clattering along the road. How he got away with it I do not know, but then we rarely saw a policeman in Ashenridge.

Bert's remark got everyone laughing, not that he or any of his friends had ever been inside the chapel.

One of Bert's pals was determined to have his five pennyworth. "They say they're taking out all the pews *and* the pulpit *and* the organ and having a stage instead with a cinema screen and pop groups."

That caused more laughter.

"And flashing lights and some sort of restaurant with a bar."

"They Methodies. They talk about being temporal, why they'm the biggest 'ippocrites out."

"Did you hear about poor old Mr Braddle and his missus? They've given up chapel after going there for nigh on sixty years. It's a crying shame."

"And they're not the only ones. They say most of the old folk are leaving."

Jim Stillman had been quietly listening from the other end of the bar. "For what it's worth, if they go on like this they'll be putting the poor old Coach and Horses out of business."

"Wouldn't fancy having a pint there. Bet they'd know how to charge."

Bert was beginning to wish he hadn't started all of this.

"Giddon, you'm making it up. They'd never do all that. What do you reckon, rector?"

All eyes turned on me. "Well, you know how people exaggerate. I suspect there's very little truth in what you've been saying."

* *

In fact I knew much more about what was happening at the chapel than I was prepared to let on. I did not wish to takes sides over an issue which deeply divided the local church and the Methodists. It all started when a family by the name of Armstrong moved into a cottage in the centre of the village.

"They've only been here a short while, but from what I hear you would be the best person to call on them," Will Swift had stated at a staff meeting.

Will, Henry Burrows and Sonia Williams had all been doing their best to call on any newcomers, but some were less easy than others. "Leave any difficult ones to me," I'd foolishly suggested.

I called at Way Cottage wondering just what sort of a reception I'd receive. I was usually given a friendly welcome wherever I called, even if the people concerned never intended darkening the inside of a church. A new breed of town people moving into the villages was generally pleased, if a little surprised, to see me. Others showed polite indifference.

An unsmiling Mrs Armstrong opened the door. She didn't invite me in straight away, but when I mentioned that someone from the church always tried to welcome newcomers she called out to her husband. He told his wife he would deal with it and she obediently walked away.

His handshake was warm enough, but there was no mistaking the hint of disdain in his voice. "Strange, we've lived here for over three months now and haven't seen a soul from the church."

Before I had chance to offer any kind of explanation I found myself being marched through the house.

I'd been inside Way Cottage many times before but I hardly recognised it now. Gone were the comfy chairs, the handmade rugs, the shelves filled with all manner of knick-knacks, even the magnificent inglenook fireplace. Instead the room was sparsely furnished with a black table and matching chairs and two black and white sofas. A huge television in one corner dominated the room. The few pictures on the wall were so abstract they meant nothing to me. In fact it was so modern I wondered why the new owners had bothered to buy an old cottage.

Three children sat on the floor playing dominoes. Mr Armstrong told them in a severe voice to end their game and greet me. They jumped to their feet, scattering the dominoes as they went. I was embarrassed by this rather unfortunate introduction and would like to have helped the children put their wooden pieces back in order, but next minute I was being led into a conservatory. This must have been a recent addition and I complimented Mr Armstrong on it. He insisted it was not a conservatory but a garden room. How strange, I thought, there wasn't a plant in sight! He used this room as his study and, like the main room, it had a contemporary feel to it. A dozen or so large, expensive-looking books, mostly on art and architecture, were neatly arranged on a long, low table.

Sensing I was letting myself in for some sort of heavy session, I tried to lighten things by reiterating I had simply called to welcome the family to Ashenridge. I added they would be made most welcome at our church.

My innocuous statement seemed to stiffen the resolve of this rather strange man. He pointed to a plastic seat then sat opposite me on the other side of a glass-topped desk.

We sat in silence, taking each other in. I imagined him to be in his mid-thirties, a slight man with receding ginger hair. He wore a neat black suit, collar and tie. He looked very much the professional type.

The awkward silence continued. I was relieved when he broke it by clearing his throat and informing me how he and his family had looked in at the church one Saturday afternoon. He was not impressed by what he found. The notices in the porch were faded and out of date. Nowhere could he find the times of the services, not even the names of the clergy. His son had innocently swung on the lychgate and as he did so an oaf appeared and proceeded to give the boy a lecture on how to treat church property. From his description I suspected that had been Peter Eastridge.

Having got past him, they entered what they expected to be a peaceful building. They were wrong. Inside they discovered a crowd of unfriendly individuals preparing the church for that Sunday's service.

He continued. "My daughter picked up a hymn book and was merely leafing through it to see if it contained her favourite hymns. Some awful woman practically leapt on her and ordered her to leave the books alone saying she'd just tidied them. So you see, Mr Longfield, not quite what we were expecting."

Naturally I apologised and said I hoped to interest him by talking about all the good things the church did. The moment I mentioned Ashenridge Sunday School Mr Armstrong bombarded me with questions as though he were a school inspector.

What sort of influence was the church having if its members treated children as his had been treated? He wanted to know exactly what they would be taught in Sunday School, and when could he see the syllabus? How did we select the teachers? What did we teach about other religions?

He then went on to ask about the religious policy of the village school. When he discovered that Mr Newman, the headmaster, was a Quaker, he looked concerned and wanted to know to what extent the children were being influenced by his ideas?

I was able to assure Mr Armstrong that the children at Ashenridge Primary School were not necessarily pacifists, if that's what he imagined.

He kept bombarding me with questions. No sooner had I answered one he came back at me with another. He gave me little chance to say anything, but I did discover one thing, he was an architect. I'd like to have learned more, but glancing at his watch he informed me he had to rush off to a business meeting in Leighford.

He led me to the front door, past the children who, once again, were seated on the floor, this time watching television.

It would not have surprised me one bit if the picture had been in black and white!

* *

The following Sunday the Armstrongs were sitting in Ashenridge Church, a good fifteen minutes before the service was due to begin. Unfortunately they had chosen the early morning Communion Service, always the quietest one of the month. Eventually a few elderly people joined them, but when they went up to receive Communion the Armstrongs remained firmly in their pew. From the stony look on Mr Armstrong's face I suspected it would be the first and last time we saw them in Ashenridge Church.

The following Sunday the family attended the service at Ashenridge Chapel. The congregation there wasn't that big either, but after the service everyone gathered round the Armstrongs and made them feel most welcome, so welcome that Mr Armstrong declared it was the first friendly church in the area he had come across. How different from the parish church and those they had tried in Leighford. Since this chapel seemed to suit his family best he stated they would continue to worship there, although he couldn't resist adding that their heating system was outdated, the damp on the walls a matter of some concern, and the hymns sung that Sunday were not to his liking.

If the welcome the Armstrongs received elsewhere had been perceived by them as chilly, the Methodists were soon beginning to wonder if theirs had been a bit too warm.

I had to admit I was actually relieved not to have a highly opinionated Mr Armstrong breathing down my neck, but all the same I was a little concerned as to how the Methodists would cope with him. They were open, friendly people, and I did not want the pleasant atmosphere at the chapel to be spoilt.

A few weeks later I heard that the Methodist organist was unwell and Mr Armstrong had offered to play in her absence. Next thing we knew he'd more or less taken over every decision concerning the hymns. Even Wesley Peterson was struggling to choose the hymns he wanted. When the regular organist recovered, Mr Armstrong made her feel so unwelcome she gladly handed everything over to him.

So far I had kept out of things. It was not my place to interfere. But then our Sunday School teacher voiced her concerns. Over the last few weeks attendance had been falling and she'd heard that three more of our children had left to join the new Sunday School at the chapel. She feared more would follow.

I was glad for the Methodists that more children were going there. For years they had lacked any support from young people. If, however, it was going to lead to a mass exodus of children from Ashenridge Church that was a different matter.

"It's fine if they reach out to those youngsters who never attend," our Sunday School teacher exclaimed, "but what they're doing is tantamount to stealing children from our church."

A few nights later the matter was raised at a church council meeting. Action was required, but what? I could hardly tell the Methodists how to run their chapel, and even if I had the power to force the children to return to Ashenridge Church I would not have done so. It would more than likely have driven them away.

Wesley Peterson himself was very concerned. It transpired the Armstrongs had come from a very high-powered church in the Midlands. Mr Armstrong repeatedly stated that 'we owe it to our children to give them the very best introduction to the faith. They must be offered the best teaching, first-class facilities, and the most stimulating programme possible'. He did not mind where the children came from. If it involved poaching all the church children, so be it. He also had plans to transform the little Victorian chapel into something worthy of the twentieth century. This included replacing all the hard pews with movable seats, and turning the back of the chapel into a kitchen and toilets. The ceiling was quite high, so he planned to create a gallery over the kitchen for Sunday School and youth work. There would be shutters between the gallery and the main chapel which, on special occasions, could be drawn back allowing some of the congregation to sit there yet still join in the service below.

Such ideas were creating deep divisions. Some of the older members were making noises about leaving and indeed some of them, like Mr and Mrs Braddle, had already done so. They were distressed to see the building they'd loved for most of their lives being changed so dramatically. But at the same time Mr Armstrong's ideas were being supported by families who had never been inside the building before.

Wesley was wondering how long this Sunday School would last. Mr Armstrong was too much of a disciplinarian and his wife too weak for either of them to earn proper respect from the children. It was true, one or two children from our Sunday School had joined them and Wesley felt uneasy about it. Like me, he believed they should be trying to reach those children who never went anywhere near a church or a chapel. He did, however, like the plans for refurbishing the chapel. He felt that even if some of Mr Armstrong's other ideas never came to fruition, they would at least have a building which would benefit everyone, Methodist or Anglican. I agreed with him.

Unfortunately, in a village tongues will wag. While I tried to reassure our churchgoers that the chapel was not planning a take-over of all the village youth, a very different version of this got back to Mr Armstrong. He was told that Wesley and I had put our heads together and watered down all his ideas.

This resulted in a warlike Mr Armstrong coming to see me. Knowing something of his style, I insisted that if he had something important to say it was no good him expecting an instant response. He must allow time for me to consider his points.

He looked slightly taken aback.

"Peace at any price, is that it? All you and Wesley Peterson want is to play for time, totally ignoring a new generation that is looking for the light. To keep the peace, you pander to the faithful few who still come to your services. Soon they'll all be gone, and then you'll have nothing left. I'm offering new wine, all you can offer is old bottles."

"What are you proposing, Mr Armstrong? Turning our churches into some kind of Butlins? Will it be entertainment instead of a cross? Churches competing with each other instead of uniting to bring faith to the community?"

"Not at all, but you and the Methodists must admit that what you're doing here isn't cutting any ice. My family gets told off for even daring to put its nose inside your church. Then we come to your service and find half a dozen old folk using some ancient rite which nobody can understand. We go to chapel and sit on hard seats, listening to a verbose preacher, and then we sing dull hymns. Two churches in one village doing more or less the same thing for the benefit of the few elderly people who attend. What hope in hell has either of making an impact on today's world? At least the Methodists are prepared to listen to me."

"So what do you have in mind?" I asked.

"Up until two years ago I never went to church. Then I came across a really lively one in the West Midlands. Their building was bright and modern, their cheerful music appealed to everyone. Their services were up to date, bright and challenging. And they did all manner of things for young people. It changed my life."

"It's a pity you didn't come to our church for the next Family Service. You'd have seen a fair number of youngsters doing just the sort of thing you've talked about. It would have been the same last week if you hadn't drawn some of our families away.

"A lot more happens here about which you know nothing. My lay team and helpers have recommenced the praise and prayer services. Attendance is growing. And another thing, at least a quarter of the population of this parish are seen sometimes at services in church or chapel, and that's a very conservative estimate."

A flicker of surprise crossed his face, but I didn't want him to interrupt me.

"I like your plans to modernise the chapel. If two churches are to survive in the village they need to feel very different. One traditional, the other modern. If your ideas come off I'm sure everyone will benefit. There's just one thing you have to realise. In a big place, like the town you came from, the population is large enough for each church to work independently. In a small place like

129

this your ideas will only bear fruit if the two work together."

Mr Armstrong may not have liked everything I said, but at least he agreed to bear my words in mind.

It was only the following summer, when he saw all the children at our Holiday Club, Mr Armstrong began to appreciate that he did not have a monopoly on youth work.

* *

The refurbishing of the chapel inevitably created much pain for those who had loved the old building from childhood. The Methodists shared our church building for many months while work continued on the chapel. This had the effect of bringing two congregations closer together. Sometimes we united for services, sometimes we held separate ones. On both sides give and take was paramount.

As a further measure of this new relationship, that May the local Methodists and Anglicans shared a bus and travelled to Bristol for one of Billy Graham's Mission England meetings. It was a huge success.

Ironically, before the work on the chapel was completed, the Armstrong family moved away, something everyone viewed with mixed feelings. They returned to Ashenridge for the re-dedication of the chapel. When the service was over the chairs were placed round the walls and tables, laden with food, spread across the centre of the chapel. I found myself talking to a much more relaxed Mr Armstrong. He told me that most of his work in East Anglia involved church restoration. I wondered how he was getting on with the clergy there.

A day or two later I paid a lunch-time visit to the Coach and Horses. Once again the subject came round to the chapel.

"They say 'tis a proper job. A bit of competition for you, eh, rector?" asked Bert Bending with a twinkle in his eye.

"I tell you this, they certainly have done a good job, something we can all benefit from. In fact next Monday I'm officiating at a funeral in the church and after the service there's a get-together in the chapel for tea. As you're one of the deceased's cousins, Bert, I'll expect you to be there. Then you can judge for yourself."

This stopped Bert in his tracks.

"Yurr, Bert," someone else commented. "Pity that Mr Hamstring, or whatever 'is name was, didd'n 'ave a go at transformin' your car. I see your number plate's fallen off altogether now."

"Giddon," said Bertie. "You'm 'avin me on."

Chapter 13

The Badger Group Christmas Party

It was mid-November and a group of willing helpers were out and about delivering copies of the Badger News to all six parishes with details of the Christmas party.

For many this gathering was one of the highlights of their year and people were quick to make a note of it in their diary for the second Saturday in December.

The programme was much the same as in previous years. Light refreshments would be provided, although this year the Badger News and the posters requested that everyone bring along a plate of sandwiches. Mary had been busy organising the fun quiz, which Will Swift always won. Then the grand draw would take place followed by a medley of carols to round off the evening.

An hour or so before the party I popped into the village hall where some of the committee were already busy preparing for the evening ahead. I went back to Mary full of admiration. I'd never seen the hall looking so good.

People began arriving early, eager to grab a seat. The formidable Mrs Mathilda Pink, whose job it had been to organise the notice in the Badger News as well as the posters, was dismayed to see so many people turning up with a plate of sandwiches.

As more and more sandwiches were placed on the refreshments table she turned to Annie Cook with a look of panic on her face.

"This is dreadful, Annie. I specifically requested a plate of sandwiches *or* home-made mince pies. So where are the mince pies?" Her voice had risen to a crescendo and someone had to put the poor lady out of her misery.

"You only asked for a plate of sandwiches, and that's what you've got, dear. Look at your poster. No mention of mince pies anywhere. The same applies to the Badger News."

Mrs Pink's cheeks turned a funny sort of beetroot colour as she stared at the poster. Despite all her careful checking she could now see that one vital line had been omitted. No wonder the refreshments table was groaning under a mountain of sandwiches.

It was Mr Radd who saved the day. He quickly dashed to his shop and returned with ten boxes of Mr Kipling mince pies. They may not have been home made, but a relieved Mrs Pink found herself joining in the laughter as everyone agreed that Mr Kipling did indeed make exceedingly good cakes.

I caught sight of Kitty, one of the oldest parishioners in Ashenridge. She didn't get out much these days, but

Mabel Waterhead had made sure she didn't miss this event. Having lost her teeth years ago, and having thrown her false set away, she still managed to tuck into a turkey sandwich, leaving a neat pile of crusts on the side of her plate.

After a third glass of mulled wine Kitty's voice was growing louder and louder. A minute or two later there was complete silence as she slumped back in her chair fast asleep. She remained like that until the raffle.

Mabel and Sonia were busy selling raffle tickets. They'd gone to a lot of trouble collecting the prizes which were displayed on a table beside the Christmas tree. Boxes of chocolates, bottles of wine, some of them home made, jars of chutney, a Christmas cake, boxes of crackers, and more, surrounded a hand-made Christmas voucher picturing a Bronze Turkey. This was the star prize, donated by a local farmer and guaranteed to be delivered to the winner in good time for Christmas. No wonder the raffle tickets were selling like hot cakes.

* *

The fun quiz was just that, with people simply raising their hands if they knew the answers. Mary called out the questions from the stage and the response was impressive. With only one question to go Will and Max were running neck and neck, but it was Will who knew the final answer and was declared the winner.

I spent a few minutes taking in the scene before me. It warmed my heart to see everyone having such a good time. All six parishes were there in force, including folk from Ashenridge Chapel. I wished our dear friends, Stephanie and Henry Burrows, could have been with us, but they were attending a Christmas event at the cathedral, which happened to fall on the same evening. As for Uncle Tiddly, he'd have loved this party, but we hadn't heard from him in ages. He professed to being semi-retired, but still disappeared for months on end intent on making a fortune.

* *

There was a bit of a kerfuffle going on at one end of the hall. Peter Eastridge and Will Swift were obviously experiencing some difficulty giving Len Cooksley a fireman's lift on to the stage. They handed him his walking sticks, made sure he'd got his bearings, and Peter announced that our good friend had a bit of a surprise for us. All eyes were on Len, who endeavoured to speak in a Sunday voice. "Good heevening, ladies and gentlemen, and you too rector. This here is one of my favourite poems, and I wants to share it with you. It is called *The Better Plan* and 'tis – sorry, it is – by someone

who goes by the name of William Weeks. I hopes you
likes it. Here goes."

Young Tom, the farmer's, man, one night
Was going down the lane,
Candle and lantern in his hand,
To meet his Mary Jane

Now, as it happen'd, farmer Giles
Was coming up the lane,
And meeting Tom with lantern asked:
"Why, Tom, where be 'ee gwain?"

Tom, looking sheepish, answered, "Zur,
Sure you knaw where I'm gwain –
'Tis courtin' night an' I'm jist off
To meet my Mary Jane"

"But take a lantern courtin', Tom!
You be a quare young spark!
I always thort that sort o' thing
Was better in the dark."

"Wull, maister, I 'ave always yerd
'Tis var the safest plan
To thraw some light 'pon anything
That you may take in 'an."

"Fudge! I'd no light to court my wive
When 'er was Nancy Ridd."
Sez Tom: "To jidge by the looks o' 'er,
I shouldn' think you did!"

"Thank you for listenin', said Len. "I 'ope you enjoyed it 'cause I knows I did."

People were bent double with laughter, and the cheers and applause continued as Will and Peter helped Len back to his seat. A crowd gathered round wanting to know if Len could give a repeat performance at next year's party.

"Well, I ain't givin' any promises. I'm a bit long in the tooth now and I can't go on…" Len was struggling to find the right words.

Annie thought she knew what he meant. "For ever."

"No, Annie, but you'm close. What I wants to say is I can't go on adding…"

"Adding fuel to the fire," one bright spark suggested.

"No, no, no." Len turned to me. "Rector, you'm sure to know what I mean. I can't go on adding…"

"I think what you're trying to say, Len, is you can't go on *ad infinitum*. Am I right?"

"That's the one, rector. I can't go on *adding finitum*."

Len was chuckling to himself as he turned to me again. "Cor, you'm a dark horse ain't you, rector? Us didd'n know you could speak French!"

It was time for the raffle and there was something of a scramble as several rushed to buy extra tickets. And who could blame them? The prizes this year were the best I'd ever seen. I bought a couple of extra tickets myself and handed one to Mary. "There you are, my dear," I said jokingly. "That's sure to be a winner."

Mary laughed. "It's years since I won a raffle prize. It was a plastic doll, and it gave me the creeps. Its eyes used to follow me round and I ended up putting it in the spare bedroom. I wonder what happened to it?"

Miss Prince, one of the churchwardens at South Monkton, had been given the happy task of drawing the winning tickets.

"As you know," she said, vigorously shaking a large plastic bucket and plunging her arm deep into it, "tonight's star prize is a Bronze Turkey and the winning ticket is…" Here Miss Prince paused for affect, waving a ticket in the air. "The winning ticket is a pink one, number 43."

I was holding pink ticket number 44 which meant Mary must have ticket number 43, although of course she might have ticket number 45. I couldn't be sure.

I saw Mary walking towards the raffle table and watched proudly as she collected the voucher. There was a ripple of applause, quickly followed by a lot of laughter from the back of the hall, where someone had started telling jokes. A few of those sitting nearby were happily joining in.

"Have you heard this one? Who's never hungry at Christmas?"

"Don't know," several yelled back. "Who is never hungry at Christmas?"

"The turkey, cause he's stuffed!"

This brought a good round of laughter, but by now Miss Prince was losing her composure and it was Peter Eastridge who came to the rescue. "C'mon, lads," he shouted. "Let this good lady get on or us'll be 'ere all night."

His loud voice woke Kitty with such a start she nearly missed hearing her own number being called. She'd won two boxes of assorted toffees, which she promptly handed to Len, who handed them to Annie, who tucked them in her handbag because of the three of them she was the only one who still had her own teeth.

* *

It was a firm tradition in Ashenridge that we round off the evening with carols. This year we'd invited each of the five other parishes to choose one of their favourites. Annie handed out the song sheets, and Miss Prince was seated at the piano, eager to start playing.

We began with Once in Royal David's City followed by The First Noel. Then came Silent Night and Ding Dong Merrily on High.

The final carol was Hark! The Herald Angels Sing and as we sang Glory to the new born King for the last time someone switched off the hall lights and dozens of red and gold candles flickered around us.

Kitty was making for the door and Mabel called out to her: "Wait there and I'll see you get home safely." Kitty was humming a familiar Christmas song. "One of me favourites that one." She gave me a wistful smile. "Bing Crosby, 'e used to sing it." Her frail voice was barely audible as she remembered the words: 'I'm dreaming of a white Christmas, just like the ones I used to know…'

Mary and I linked arms and walked back towards the rectory. A full moon lit our way and, as though reflecting the fairy lights here on earth, a multitude of stars twinkled from millions of light years away.

Max had come along with us and seemed preoccupied. "What are you thinking?" I asked him.

"Do you know, Jack, I don't think I've ever come across such happiness as I found tonight. I've been to numerous parties, but nothing like this. I always thought church people were a bit dull and miserable. Now I know better. You might even see me in church one day."

We wished Max goodnight. I couldn't help feeling a twinge of sadness as I watched him returning alone to Laburnum Lodge. He'd once confided in me how much he'd suffered when his childhood sweetheart broke off their engagement, only two months before they were due to be married. Maybe one day he would let another woman into his life – he might even meet someone in one of our churches.

Mary was still clutching the prize-winning voucher and gave a deep sigh. "I still can't believe I won first prize, Jack. I'd been planning to buy a turkey in Leighford next week. It was at the top of my shopping list."

Our good fortune didn't end there because the very next day we had a telephone call from Uncle Tiddly saying he'd love to accept our invitation to spend Christmas and the New Year with us.

And the good news continued because for the first time in three years our son-in-law, Harry, had managed to get cover for his parishes. This meant that he, Ann and the twins would be with us for lunch on Christmas Day and could stay at the rectory for a few nights.

"I've got a funny feeling this Christmas is going to be a bit special, Jack. It's a long time since we've had a full house at the rectory." Mary started laughing. "And that turkey's going to come in pretty handy."

"Absolutely," I agreed. "Let's ask Max to come over and share it with us."

Chapter 14

Give Peace a Chance

I sat at one end of the kitchen table feeling utterly miserable. Mary was serving Sunday lunch, our favourite meal of the week. I had just got home having taken a lacklustre Communion Service at North Monkton Church. That morning the service had seemed totally flat. I felt we had simply gone through the motions of worship and nothing more.

Most North Monkton folk preferred the easy-going family services which took place on the other Sundays of the month. Will Swift or Sonia Williams usually led them, and recently they had been encouraging members of the congregation to play a bigger part.

"It's the only way for small churches to survive," Will maintained. In many ways he was right. With fewer clergy the congregations of the future would probably have to take more services on their own. This was a fine idea in theory, but it made no allowance for someone like Stan Forward, a well-meaning but rather forceful newcomer to the village.

Recently the parish had been taken by surprise when James Smallcott resigned as churchwarden. This came about as a result of his meeting the archdeacon. With some pride James had told him how he'd held the office of churchwarden for over twenty years. Instead of receiving the expected praise, a shocked James was informed that ten years as churchwarden was quite long enough. He resigned on the spot.

Stan Forward had seemed to be the obvious replacement. His credentials were excellent, although the vicar at his former parish had conveniently forgotten to mention he was an ardent member of the Campaign for Nuclear Disarmament *and* the Christian CND. He had no qualms about bringing his beliefs into the church, and usually gave them priority when we invited him to lead the prayers.

He wore a CND badge in his left lapel, a CCND on the right, this one portraying a dove holding an olive branch in its beak, which Stan repeatedly advised everyone was a 'true symbol of peace'.

"I was at the demonstration in 1981, one of the biggest you've ever seen. Thousands marched through London that day, and it took us five hours. I'd never seen such a crowd. Tony Benn *and* Michael Foot were there."

* *

Roast beef and Yorkshire pudding – my favourite lunch smiled up at me from my plate. Mary was already tucking into hers, but having jumped on to my proverbial soapbox I now found myself unable to stop talking.

"When we re-opened North Monkton things were so different. The bright simple services we held brought the whole parish together. Yet even then some prophets of doom thought it was a nine-day wonder. I had a congregation of eight this morning, and one of them was a baby. I'm told the congregation's no better at South Monkton."

"Why don't you eat your lunch, Jack. We can talk about it later."

"There was a dreadful atmosphere. You remember Betty Burnell and Ada Ashwell, the two sisters. Well, they sat in the same pew but completely ignored each other. Mrs King sat behind them with a self-satisfied grin on her face. And a cheerless Mrs Smallcott played hymns on an organ which badly needs tuning. As for Stan Forward, he was more interested in showing off his ban the bomb badges as he handed out the new service booklets he's forced upon us."

"Do eat your lunch, Jack. It's going cold."

"To make things worse, a young couple sat in the back pew holding a baby who cried on and off for the rest of the service. I ask you, Mary, why on earth do newcomers always come to the least well attended services?"

"Don't let your lunch go cold, dear."

"What they witnessed must have confirmed their worst suspicions – a handful of elderly people in a near-empty church. I'm sure we'll never see them again. They couldn't get away quickly enough."

Mary gave me a resigned look. "Don't forget, Jack, in the old days, before the church was closed, the congregation never amounted to more than six or seven. What's more, you know very well that most North Monkton people still prefer their free and easy services. When you take one of those you always come home saying how much you've enjoyed it. It's a pity that on half a word from the church Stan Forward rushed out and bought those modern service booklets. Most of the congregation don't know where they are. You'll have to be firm with 'Ban-the-Bomb Stan'. You're the rector. If you're not careful he'll drive people away with his strong views."

As she finished speaking Mary banged her knife and fork down on to her empty plate with such force it gave me quite a start.

"For heaven's sake, Jack, will you *please* eat your lunch."

* *

A few days later I took a phone call from a young woman by the name of Deborah. She explained she was the same woman I had seen in church, and asked if she could come and see me because she and her husband, Edward, were hoping to have their baby baptised at North Monkton Church.

We chatted over a cup of tea in the drawing-room. "You don't remember me do you, Mr Longfield? I was the one who knew all the answers to your questions at family services."

I suddenly remembered that bright, enthusiastic face. She was the girl who always put her hand up first. That must have been a good ten years ago.

We reminisced about the past and she explained that her mother still lived on the farm, but since the death of her husband she needed more and more help.

"Edward and I are planning to return to North Monkton, to live in a converted barn on the old family farm. Edward's worked on his father's farm since he was a young boy so he'll be able to help my mother, and it'll be lovely for her having Serenity next door.

"Serenity. What a beautiful name."

"Yes. When I was expecting, Mum bought me a book of baby names. For years Dad's favourite expression had been 'give me a bit of peace', and when we saw that Serenity meant peace it seemed like a sort of tribute to him. If we'd had a boy we'd have called him Oliver."

Deborah looked down at the sleeping baby, and for a moment she looked sad.

"But there are problems. Edward's not at all sure if North Monkton is the right church for the baby's baptism."

"Do you know why?"

"I do. He came along to the church knowing you would be taking the Communion Service. He wanted to get an idea of what the church is like. And, to be honest, he wanted to listen to your sermon, to get an idea of what you are like."

"Did I make a terrible hash of it?"

"No. It wasn't your fault, but to be honest neither of us felt very comfortable. It wasn't just that we felt a bit awkward when you invited us to come up for a blessing while the others received communion. There really was an awful atmosphere in the church. Edward was upset that even the words to the Lord's Prayer had been changed. They weren't the ones he'd learnt at school."

"Oh, dear," I thought, "Stan Forward's influence again."

Deborah continued: "I tried explaining to Edward that not all services are the same. You see, he's never been one for going to church and it's not easy for him to understand."

"So, will you have Serenity baptised somewhere else?"

"I don't want that. We'll be living in the parish before very long. And there was something you said in your sermon that's got Edward thinking. We didn't catch all of it, and I'm sorry if Serenity's crying got a bit much, but it was something to do with shaking hands."

I knew exactly what Deborah was talking about. I'd recounted the story of how I'd once unfairly criticised a fellow clergyman and soon afterwards discovered my mistake, by which time it was too late. I was dreading the next time we met and the minute I saw him I made a point of going up to him and apologising. His face lit up and he gave me the warmest of handshakes. It totally transformed my day, and at the time I was quite lost for words. It brought home to me the importance of the 'peace' handshake during a service.

"Edward said that your story made him realise that clergymen are no different to anyone else. They have the same feelings, make the same mistakes. I'm not sure what he imagined they were like before."

Up until then Serenity had been sleeping peacefully in her mother's arms. She now started sniffling and within seconds her sniffling turned into an almighty howl. Deborah gently rocked her and asked if it was okay to feed her. For one alarming moment I thought she was going to breastfeed the baby in front of me, but she reached into her bag and pulled out a baby's bottle and within seconds peace was restored.

"And there's another problem, rector. Ada Ashwell and Betty Burnell. I saw them shake hands at your service, but that didn't mean a thing you know. They're my mother's sisters, my aunts, but they've been at loggerheads for years. If we decide to have Serenity baptised at North Monkton I know they'll be quarrelling over who's going to do this and who's going to do that. There's sure to be trouble, and that's the last thing I want. Mum's got enough on her plate right now, especially with her health problems."

"How did all this come about? They must have been on good terms once."

"I think it's because everything seems to go well for Aunty Ada and Uncle Arthur, but nothing ever goes right for poor Aunty Betty and Uncle Ben. Uncle Arthur always got the best prices at market. His house is full of trophies he's won for showing his cattle. When he sold the farm he used the money to start up a small supermarket. It's done well, but it's made a lot of people round here jealous. Even worse, he won't buy local food. Says he can get it cheaper from abroad, and that's upset everyone as well.

"Aunt Ada dresses in smart clothes and mixes with the smart people in town. She may look a little hard, but underneath I know she's kind. She really does try to get on with Aunty Betty, but whatever she does or says is always taken the wrong way. When it comes to the church, mum says that one year Aunty Ada was asked to decorate the font – I think it was for a baptism. Aunty Betty was asked to provide a tiny floral decoration for the altar. She was really put out. Word got round, and on the next occasion they were asked to do a swap. Aunty Betty said she wasn't going to be placated like that. So you see, you just can't win."

"Yes," I agreed. "I can't see any way out of this for the moment. Tell me, when are you planning to have Serenity baptised?"

"We'll be living in the barn by September. Would that be a good time?"

"Well, that gives us a good six months. For the moment Serenity's baptism will go to the top of my prayer list."

* *

I raised the matter at our next staff meeting and Will told me something I had not realised. Mrs King was yet another aunt. Will was sure that behind the scenes she had been working hard to encourage the couple to have the baptism at North Monkton. No wonder she had looked so pleased when Deborah and Edward attended the service.

North Monkton had previously been cared for by one of my fellow clergy which meant I did not know the people there that well. I felt the time was right to visit the Ashwells and the Burnells, but experience had taught me to be cautious and feel my way rather than rush headlong into a situation.

The Ashwells treated me like royalty. Ada called her husband in from the garage where he'd been polishing his vintage car. I was shown into an elegantly furnished drawing-room where an incredible collection of trophies stood on a mahogany sideboard. Arthur explained how some of them had been won. That, of course, was while he was still farming.

He was about to start talking about his supermarket when Ada, perhaps sensing trouble, quickly changed the subject to her orchids. She had a superb show of them in the conservatory, which now acted as an extension to the room we were sitting in. She did not say where all the plants had come from, but I guessed it was the garden section of their very own supermarket.

As I left I thought how things had changed from the modest farmhouse it had been when I called there many years ago. The drive alone had obviously had a fortune spent on it, but I was surprised at the poor state of the hedges leading up to it. Sheep had broken through several gaps and could be seen wandering freely along the surrounding lanes.

Later that day I drove down a track to the Burnells' farm. The surface here was rough and bumpy, but what caught my eye were the expertly laid hedges. Ben Burnell, in overalls and a greasy cap, emerged from the sheep shed. He gave me a cheery smile and led me into a homely kitchen. Lucky, his sheep dog, charged at me in welcome and Ben proudly told me about his prowess at local sheep dog trials. Judging by the number of photographs and rosettes displayed on the dresser, Lucky was indeed a champion.

Betty came in from checking the lambs and offered me 'just a cup of tea'. It was a long time coming, but the wait was more than worthwhile. Her home-made scones were still warm from the oven, the clotted cream had the crustiest top I'd ever seen, and then there were those jars filled with Betty's own delicious strawberry jam.

Over tea I told Ben how I'd been admiring his hedges. They were the best in the parish and really kept the sheep at bay, not easy in springtime before the grass has properly grown. His were a shining example to others. I purposely, and perhaps rather mischievously, mentioned that Arthur's hedges were in a sorry state. A triumphant smile crept over Ben's face.

"Well, I can tell you why that is. It's young Ronnie, the Ashwells' nephew. He farms all the land round Arthur's farm these days, but he knows nothing when it comes to keeping hedges. He thinks all you need is a flail cutter, but that's no good on a weary old hedge. It only makes it worse."

"Well," I added, "I don't think we need to look much beyond this kitchen to find the person to teach people like young Ronnie how to lay a hedge. With your hedging and dog-handling skills you've got a lot to pass on."

As I left the farm, I decided that next time I got a chance I'd have a word about hedging with the chairman of the local Young Farmers' Club. If Ben could be brought in to give some instruction it would do wonders for his ego.

A week later, Deborah and Edward were both sitting round our kitchen table drinking mugs of tea. Deborah had persuaded Edward to attend one of the friendlier and better attended North Monkton services which had finally brought him round to having Serenity baptised there. We could now go ahead and make all the necessary arrangements.

Behind the scenes two things happened to ease the bad feelings between the Burnells and the Ashwells. Ben Burnell was very pleased to be approached about demonstrating traditional hedge laying to the local Young Farmers' Club. There was even talk about him training others to go in for sheep dog trials. At the same time, and responding to criticism, the Ashwell's supermarket had begun selling locally-grown food.

Mrs King was over the moon. It looked as if everything would end happily, but life isn't like that.

All was going according to plan for the baptism. Ada Ashwell fussed around her friends as they decorated the church, and Betty Burnell was contentedly decorating the parish hall. Ada had been attending flower arranging classes. The result was that any comparison between the way in which the two ladies arranged their flowers was all too transparent. Aware of this, Ada made a point of praising her sister's floral decorations. Unfortunately she overdid it, and her honeyed words came across to Betty as patronising.

Another of Ada's well-intentioned ideas also ended in disaster. Knowing that Deborah and Edward were on a tight budget, she got all the food for the get-together in the village hall at a very generous discount – from their supermarket. Regrettably this fact leaked out.

"Cheap food for a cheap baptism," someone said in Mrs Ashwell's hearing.

"But I was only trying to help." Ada was close to tears as she left the hall.

"I suppose food from Arthur's supermarket is better than nothing," another woman muttered. "Left to the Burnells it would have been a right pig's trotter of a meal!"

Betty chanced to enter the hall at that very moment and, overhearing this remark, stomped off home in a rage.

Stirred up by what Betty had told him, Ben Burnell now twisted my words to add a little more fuel to the fire.

"Yes, and Arthur with all his money lets his hedges go wild. There are sheep wandering all over the place. You ask the rector. That's what he told me."

* *

If the atmosphere at the North Monkton service six months before had been a little tense, it was nothing compared to the poison being spread on the eve of the baptism.

The phone in my study rang. It was a tearful Deborah wanting to call the whole thing off. She and Edward did not want to have Serenity baptised with such a fuss going on.

At nine o'clock the following morning the phone rang again. It was Deborah asking if the baptism could take place after all because overnight everyone had come to their senses.

I cannot say that the baptism was without its moments, but for the sake of Deborah and Edward, and most of all for Serenity, everyone did their best. That evening Mary and I sat down quietly to reflect upon the day.

Ada Ashwell had turned up in a very showy outfit with a matching picture hat, but even so we both got the impression that she was genuinely admiring Betty's rather simple turquoise dress. And Betty was heard speaking with appreciation about the food provided by the supermarket.

A few weeks later Mary told me what she'd witnessed while shopping at Arthur Ashwell's supermarket. "Do you know who I saw chatting together in the home produce section? It was Betty Burnell and Ada Ashwell. They were doing their weekly shop together and told me they were sorry they couldn't stop for a chat because they were off to the farm to see Deborah's mum and then they'd be popping in to see Serenity."

* *

The atmosphere at North Monkton's next Communion Service was completely different. Ada and Betty shook hands as though they really meant it. Mrs Smallcott bravely played the organ, which still needed tuning. For once 'Ban-the-Bomb Stan' managed to restrain himself from talking non-stop about the CND. And as for Mrs King, well she had plenty to smile about.

Deborah and Edward were there, and this time their daughter slept through the whole service. Afterwards we gathered at the back of the church for a chat and each of the ladies took it in turn to cuddle a still sleeping Serenity.

There might only have been a congregation of eight that Sunday, but this time the service came alive to me because I now knew everyone so much better.

"Remember what you said about the service you took at North Monkton all those months ago," said Mary. "Don't make that mistake again, Jack. Much more was happening on that occasion than you realised."

"True," I replied. "But now I hear 'Ban-the-Bomb Stan' wants another of his 'peace' services at North Monkton. That's going to take some handling."

Chapter 15

Kitty

When I moved to Ashenridge in the 1950s I heard Kitty's voice long before I actually met her. She was yelling at her granddaughter, Becky, her angry voice emanating from Wishwell Cottage, a dilapidated hovel set behind a row of houses in the middle of the village.

Kitty spent most of the time caring for her elderly father and her granddaughter, Becky, whose mother had long since deserted her. I remembered Kitty telling me how she and her husband Charlie had only been married a few years when he was struck down with typhoid. Kitty hadn't had much of a life.

She did get something of a respite three or four times a week when she met up with her friends in the wooden bus shelter. The shelter had been built in the 1930s to commemorate those who fell in the Great War. The names of local men who died in the Second World War were added later.

It was in the bus shelter that I actually met Kitty, her stooped figure tucked away in the corner, a cigarette drooping from her mouth. To begin with she never spoke in my presence and could hardly manage a smile, but I persevered and several days later she spoke to me. I remember her first words as though it were yesterday. I was eager to find out her name and she'd simply replied in a quiet voice, 'Tis Kitty'. The ice had been broken, but it would be another few days before I discovered that Kitty only had the use of one arm, the left one always hanging limply at her side.

Eventually Kitty had been forced to leave Wishwell Cottage and for the past twenty-odd years had lived in a council house in Ashenridge. Mabel Waterhead had been a good neighbour, always happy to keep a close eye on her.

* *

"It was a total disaster," a tearful Sonia Williams announced. "Last Sunday the Gospel Light Group came all the way from Whiteminster to lead our youth service. They missed out on a big event in Plymouth to be here. And what greeted them – only half a dozen teenagers."

Such an admission of defeat from Sonia came as a bit of a shock. Ever since she had been involved with youth work she had always been full of hope and confidence.

"Something's gone badly wrong," she continued. "The youngsters used to be full of enthusiasm, but recently numbers have plummeted and last night was the end. At this rate our youth work will fizzle out. We must do something about it."

This we did. It was the middle of the week, and one of the wettest days of the month, when we met to talk the whole thing over. Unfortunately, everybody arrived full of gloom. Will Swift was depressed because the sheep at Leighford Market were not fetching good prices. Henry Burrows turned up late and soaking wet because on the way over he'd had to change a tyre in the pouring rain. Sonia Williams looked half asleep. Her husband had been up most of the night suffering with chest pains which frightened both of them, but thankfully turned out to be nothing worse than acute indigestion. Because of her increasing involvement with the youngsters, Mabel Waterhead was there too. That morning, however, her mind was elsewhere.

"It's Kitty," Mabel began as soon as she arrived. "She's really low. Got it into her head she's got cancer. All down to her chain smoking. Those cigarettes, they did her no good, and she knew it. It was a bit late in the day when she did give it up. Now she's getting worse and she's always short of breath. I keep going round, and so does her granddaughter, Becky. She comes over whenever she can. Only it's a fair way from Badgermouth. I asked Kitty only the other day if she prays about it and she said, 'Yes, only tidd'n doin' me no good'."

"Didn't you bring Kitty to one of those youth services a few months ago?" Will asked, trying to steer the conversation round to the purpose of the meeting. "I remember asking her what she thought of it and she grumbled about the singing being a bit too modern for her taste."

"Yes," I added. "It's great to see Kitty coming to church. She says she likes cheerful hymns. Maybe she's started coming because she's worried about having cancer. If she's at the next youth service, why don't we let her choose one or two of the hymns?"

"It really is sad about Kitty," said Mabel, completely missing my point. "The kids are upset about her being so poorly." Then pulling up her chair and warming to the subject she added: "After most of her old friends died she didn't go out much. Now she's taken to sitting in the bus shelter again on nice days, when somebody can take her there. And she's been talking to the kids. Strange how they're so fond of her. If they thought she was coming to one of their services I reckon they'd all be there."

"You know," a very damp Henry chipped in, "I think we've got it all wrong with our youngsters. That speaker from Whiteminster, the one at our deanery youth meeting, certainly stirred things up. He pointed out that Jesus didn't entertain his disciples, he sent them out to serve others. Personally, I think we try to entertain our children too much. We should be encouraging them to think about others. Young people don't have to be entertained in church, they get plenty of that elsewhere. And youngsters love raising money for good causes. Let's get them motivated. You say how much they like Kitty. Well, why not get them to put on a special service for the old folk. They could bring them along to the church and lay on cups of tea and cakes afterwards."

Henry's idea completely changed the mood of our meeting. The answer to our problem seemed so simple and Sonia and Mabel agreed to talk the whole thing over at the next youth club meeting. Much to everyone's delight the youngsters took up Henry's suggestion with real enthusiasm.

Kitty was feeling unwell on the day of the service, but she was determined not to miss it. Two members of the youth club pushed her to the church in her wheelchair. She arrived in triumph and was given place of honour in the front pew sitting next to a couple of her old friends. But my heart went out to her. She looked so frail.

Two days later Kitty was admitted to Leighford Cottage Hospital. She may have been weak in body, but the staff soon discovered she had a very strong will. She could not understand why, when she felt so ill, they made her sit in a chair for so many hours when all she wanted to do was stay in bed. She grumbled when they kept waking her to take her temperature. She was embarrassed when they asked her personal questions about her bowel movements. If only they'd spent a minute or two explaining things Kitty might have understood. As it was, one sister took an instant dislike to her and it was only later we discovered what was going on.

Most days Bill Waterhead drove his wife to the hospital, but on each visit Mabel found Kitty so sleepy and lacking any interest in life she feared the worst would happen at any moment. The sister was off-hand and insisted it was only to be expected in a woman of her age.

Eventually Kitty was transferred to Whiteminster General for further tests. I went to see her, and with a bit of gentle probing discovered what had been going on. No wonder Kitty's visitors had always found her half asleep. Just before visiting hours the sister had been giving her a sleeping tablet, probably to prevent her from making any more complaints.

Much to our surprise, and relief, a few weeks later Kitty returned home. She seemed so much better and I was glad to see a little more colour in her cheeks. Becky and Katie came over from Badgermouth and it did Kitty a power of good having her granddaughter and great-granddaughter stay with her for a few days.

* *

"Now that you're feeling more like your old self, how about coming to another of our youth services?" I asked Kitty.

"Trouble is they'm too modern for the likes of me."

"So what you would like to happen?"

"I likes somethin' I knows. Yer knows what I mean. I leaves it to yer."

To begin with the youngsters were not exactly enthusiastic about singing traditional hymns. However, by the time Sonia had talked things through with them they became more understanding. They chose 'The day thou gavest' and 'Abide with me', although these were certainly not the happiest of hymns.

"'Tweren't no good," Kitty told Mabel afterwards. "They dull old 'ymns. Fust time I comes they sings stuff with no tune and goes on and on repeatin' it, and now this. 'Twas like goin' to a funeral. Can't us 'ave some lively ones like us used to 'ave to Sunday School?"

The interest the young people showed in Kitty seemed to breathe new life into her and some of her old strength returned. On Saturdays, when it was warm enough, they pushed her to the bus shelter in her wheelchair, which had begun squeaking so badly you could hear it long before it came into sight. A few squirts of oil would have soon put it right, but no one was that bothered. As long as everyone could hear that familiar noise they knew Kitty was still out and about.

Sitting in state, Kitty held the same spell over the youngsters she'd once held over her own generation.

She had them shrieking with laughter at her stories. Her voice may have been frail, but her memory certainly wasn't. It was hardly a coincidence that after one such session a plastic chamber pot could be seen hanging from the church tower. One day a signpost at the far end of the village was dressed up to look like a scarecrow. On another occasion a home-made 'for sale' sign was erected outside the school. It was all harmless fun.

It was amazing how the litter and mess which had blighted the bus shelter for years suddenly disappeared, and any graffiti was hastily painted over by her young admirers. There seemed to be a new spirit abroad which went hand in hand with Kitty's recovery.

One autumn evening the youth club organised another service for the elderly. On this occasion, instead of having one of Sonia's usual groups, three men led the singing, one with a guitar, another with an accordion, the third with drums. The first hymn, chosen by Kitty herself, was her favourite, 'Tell me the old, old story'. It began hesitatingly because none of the youngsters knew it, but the older folk did. Their faces lit up and they raised the roof. Kitty herself was not a great singer, but she enjoyed waving her one good arm in time to the music. Soon the youngsters were joining in as heartily as anyone. The other hymns were similarly rousing ones and transformed the service for everyone. Days later you could hear the same catchy tunes being sung in the school playground.

A triumphant Kitty was wheeled home by Mabel. "That's what I always meaned," she said. "That's what I calls a service. If they'd 'ad 'ymns like they 'ad years ago I'd 'ave been there every Sunday. Still, Mabel, next time I comes 'ere 'twill be in me coffin."

* *

News of Kitty's death flashed round the village and beyond. It was Mabel who found her. "She was lying in bed, her face turned to the window, sleeping so peacefully. I thought I'd make her a nice cup of tea, like I'd done lots of times before. I put it down on the bedside table, but when I looked at her again I knew she'd gone. Kitty was dead."

On the bedside table a much-thumbed hymn book lay open at 'Tell me the old, old story'. It must have been the last thing Kitty had looked at. An inscription on the first page revealed it had been given to her by her Sunday School teacher more than eighty years ago.

Kitty had been right all along. The tests revealed she had the very early stages of lung cancer. But, thank God, she did not die from cancer. She died of old age. And, as had been her wish, she died in her own home.

Ashenridge Church was crammed for Kitty's funeral. Such had been her influence over the years that nearly every long-standing resident was there.

Becky and Freddie looked lost as they huddled in the church porch, their arms wrapped around their distraught daughter. As the mourners arrived they had many kind words for them, but nothing could stop Katie quietly sobbing, "I love you granny, don't go, I love you, granny." My heart went out to the little girl and as I passed by I gently laid my hand on the top of her bent head. Perhaps one day the four of us would sit together recalling happy times, and we'd laugh together as we recounted some of Kitty's stories. I prayed that sooner, rather than later, the family's acute feeling of sadness would fade and be replaced by a quiet acceptance.

Becky had let me know that she wanted to make her grandmother's service a celebratory one. As you would expect, we sang 'Tell me the old, old story', followed by other rousing hymns. Becky was overcome by the hearty singing and by the way in which the young people joined in. They'd been allowed to miss school for such an important occasion, and every one of them was surprised to discover that a funeral for someone who had led such a full life could be both a happy and touching occasion with surprises of its own.

The last time I visited her in hospital Kitty had told me a story which moved me so much I asked if she would prefer it to remain a secret, or whether I could one day tell it to others. She'd nodded her agreement and after a lot of careful thought I decided to relate it at her funeral.

"You will remember how Kitty seemed to know everybody's secrets. Well, she had a few secrets of her own, and I'm going to tell you one of the most important of them."

All eyes were fixed on me. "Kitty always made out that she was born with one weak arm. In fact that wasn't so. Once, when she was a tiny child, her father flew into a rage and in a moment of madness hit Kitty so hard he badly damaged her arm. No doctor was called because her mother was terrified her husband would be imprisoned for his crime, which would have meant no money coming in. Alarmed by what he'd done, and fearing he'd be found out, he moved his family and they ended up here in Ashenridge. Within months Kitty's mother was dead. Her father tried to control his temper but still had occasional lapses, as Kitty knew only too well. As she grew up she gradually gained power over him by threatening to reveal the truth.

"What she had gone through made her hate force and violence in any way, shape or form. That was why she always used her eyes and ears to learn all she could about others. She believed the tongue should be stronger than the arm. Once she said 'Kitty knows', that was it.

"Sadly, as her friends began to fade away, Kitty all but abandoned the bus shelter, and for a while she became something of a recluse. Then a new generation of young people from the church began taking an interest in her. They loved her funny ways, and they discovered something else. Hidden under Kitty's hard exterior lay a dormant faith which was re-kindled by the services laid on for the old folk.

"And there's more. Kitty was never rich, at least not in a monetary way. When she gave up her 'ciggies', she religiously saved the spare money and only recently asked me to make sure it was used for the church youth group."

I paused and looked directly at the youngsters in front of me. "She said you made her feel young again, you made her feel happy. That's something you should all be proud of."

Chapter 16

Time to Let Go

One night I had a most disturbing dream. Most of my dreams were nonsensical, but this one was different, and at the time I wondered whether it was a warning from heaven, like some of the dreams in the Bible. It happened at a time when I was feeling particularly unwell.

I dreamt about Jonathan Hopkins, that clergyman of mixed blessings, who sometimes still came over to Ashenridge to help me. In my dream he had a look of triumph on his face as he drove a bus around the villages I knew so well. On the destination board was just one word, 'CHURCH'. Evidently I had moved away and he was in charge of my old parishes. He had closed all the churches and the worshippers were instructed to congregate in his bus. He stopped at the various villages and seemed quite pleased when nobody embarked. The dream ended with a self-satisfied Jonathan basking in the sunshine beside an empty bus. It was only a dream, but it continued to haunt me.

I was still brooding over it the following morning when Henry Burrows called at the rectory. He noticed that something was troubling me and I recounted my dream. Henry gave a short laugh and dismissed it as poppycock.

I did not tell him or anyone else how weary I was feeling, nor the pressures I was facing. Mary alone knew of my problems. As rural dean I was now spending many hours dealing with problems in other parishes, and only recently the bishop had persuaded me to run a weekly training course in Whiteminster for town clergy who were contemplating working in the countryside. All this was on top of my other duties in the six parishes. Years ago I would have taken it in my stride, but now it was taking its toll.

After nearly thirty years I felt I had taken my churches as far as I could. It was time to hand over to someone else, to someone younger. I was old enough to retire and what was more I had somewhere to go. My parents had left me a tidy sum, and Mary and I had used some of the money to buy a two-bedroom cottage in a charming village some twenty miles north of Ashenridge. Mary and I had already used it as a sort of holiday home, but before I finally retired I wanted to make sure the parishes were passing into good hands. Any thought of leaving in the immediate future had been dashed when a rumour went round that Jonathan Hopkins had been implying the bishop wanted him to take over. This was probably wishful thinking on his part, but I could not be certain.

* *

One minute I was enjoying lunch with the archdeacon, the next I'd collapsed. I have vague memories of being carted off in an ambulance and of being moved from one department to another in hospital, but there was nothing vague about the specialist's diagnosis. I'd suffered a heart attack.

On my discharge from hospital Mary was given strict instructions by the doctors *and* the bishop to take me away for a holiday, and there was an obvious place for us to go – to Paul and Emily's home in Africa.

Paul and Emily had married while Paul was still in England completing his teacher training course. Then they returned to Africa and now had a baby boy, Michael. They'd repeatedly asked us to visit them and when they heard about my heart attack they rang saying they wouldn't take 'no' for an answer. We didn't hesitate. Not only would this get me right away from my work, it would be a golden opportunity for us to see our grandson.

Mary and baby Michael were inseparable, and we spent four glorious weeks enjoying the rich customs of Kenya and its fantastic wildlife. Emily's radiant faith had changed Paul's outlook completely. Now he was not only teaching, but also spending many hours helping to rebuild the lives of children and their parents who had been so terribly traumatised by war.

Before going to Africa Paul had been an occasional churchgoer, and it had been the same when he first went to Africa, but now he and Emily loved attending their local church. Naturally this filled me with a lot of joy, and we chatted about it. "I think you were afraid I didn't believe, Dad, but nothing could be further from the truth. I just needed to work out my faith for myself and it took rather a long time."

When we arrived back in England we didn't return to the rectory straight away. We went to Greenbank Cottage. It was already beginning to feel like home and Mary and I spent the next few weeks there enjoying our new surroundings. Any talk about the parishes remained a forbidden subject. Then, as the time for my return to work approached, news of what had been going on filtered through. In my absence the bishop had indeed asked Jonathan Hopkins to come over to Ashenridge and hold the fort.

* *

Shortly before my return to the rectory Henry Burrows came to see me, bringing with him a mountain of post he'd collected from the rectory. I was alarmed by one particular letter from The Leighford Motor Traction Company saying they would be happy for me to hire a bus each Sunday morning, but I would have to pay extra insurance because it was not covered for use as a church. As I carried on reading the truth dawned. The Leighford Motor Traction Company, my foot! That letter bore all the marks of the Henry Burrows fun factory. Seconds later I saw Henry's face contorted in laughter and knew I'd guessed right.

Henry still refused to be drawn on exactly what had been going on during my absence except to say that Jonathan Hopkins was 'slowly learning'. Not entirely convinced, I made it clear to Mary I would be far better off knowing the truth.

It was at this point our daughter and son-in-law paid a brief visit. Ann and Harry had been worried sick about my poor health and proceeded to make a great fuss of me, as did the grandchildren. It did me a power of good having them stay for a few days and I let them know how much I loved them for their concern.

Not so many years ago, when he was my curate, I'd very nearly sacked Harry. He'd completely forgotten a grieving family and the funeral he was supposed to be taking. Then there was his untidiness and totally unruly hair. I'd been sorely tempted to take a brush to it many a time. I looked at Harry now. His mop of hair hadn't changed, and I was glad. It had somehow become a sort of trademark. In the end this rather scatter-brained young man had not only become my son-in-law but also a very successful country rector. It had been a joy to go and see his lively, active churches. The tables were turned now and it was up to Harry to try to sort me out.

"The trouble with you, Jack, is that you've forgotten how to relax. When I was your curate I used to love wandering down to the river. Gazing into its flowing waters I was in a different world, I was at peace and could forget my problems for a while. I didn't just go there to fish or watch birds. I prayed. I opened my mind to God, and then I went calmly on my way leaving my problems with Him. Goodness knows I did that enough times when I was trying to sort out the problems with my parents. In the end things came right and over the years they've come to accept how much I love my work.

"You sit here constantly worrying about your churches and you get yourself in such a state about your successor. No wonder things have been getting you down. One day you really will have to hand everything back to God and trust in Him. After all, it's His work as well, not just yours."

I knew Harry was right. If only I could hand over to someone like him.

"Remember," Harry continued, "I learnt a lot by my mistakes. Even if Jonathan does take over, in the end he'll learn by his mistakes, just like I did."

"That's all very well, Harry, but it takes years to build up a church. Passed into the wrong hands all of that can be destroyed in a matter of months."

* *

Peter Eastridge was on my doorstep the moment he heard I was back. His news reminded me of the frightening dream I'd had all those months ago, the details of which were still vivid.

"Darndest laziest parson I ever knowed that 'Opkins," Peter declared, his face turning red with anger. "All 'e wanted was one service on a Sunday. Didn' mind if nobody came, and 'e didn' want no 'elpers. Said they 'elpers made too much work for 'im. Told Will Swift and the others 'e didn't want they. So most churchgoers spent the day at 'ome, and the families that'd just started goin' to their own churches gived up. And they kids that used to come to what Sonia and they others put on, now they'm 'anging round again in the village in the evenings with nothin' to do. The church turned its back on the people it was supposed to be servin'. They'm our churches, not 'Opkins'. All I can say is you'm the best rector us ever 'ad, and I'm sorry I ever said otherwise."

I was trying to think of something suitable to say but Peter hadn't finished. "Then one day 'e changed. 'Twas April Fool's Day and someone put up a notice on each church door sayin' in future there'd be a bus come round and we could all worship in that. 'Opkins went wild."

"What happened?"

"Well, we 'ad a meeting. We told 'im that if 'e went on like that there'd soon be no churches. Then when 'e saw 'ow unpopular 'e was gettin' 'e said we could 'ave a service in each church every week, only 'e wouldn't be takin' 'em all. 'E takes two and wanted Will Swift and the rest to do the others. Then if they was tied up the churchwardens 'ad to do it. Told 'im I wouldn', so 'Ban-the-Bomb Stan' keeps comin' over 'ere, and 'tis drivin' everyone away."

I went straight round to see Will and Sonia who confirmed what Peter had told me. During my absence Will had in fact been invited to preach elsewhere and Sonia was having serious thoughts about going back to her old church. Will was particularly upset because, as he said, over the years we had decided just what sort of worship was right for each church and built up a team of helpers to carry out those decisions. In the name of progress Jonathan had destroyed much of our good work. He'd got rid of the helpers and put on just one service, a service that suited him with no regard for anyone else. Then suddenly it was all change and, having lost the regular leaders, he was expecting untrained people to take the services.

Henry Burrows made light of it. "Guess who put up those notices on April Fool's Day? Jonathan Hopkins may have been furious about them, but at least they got him thinking."

When I got the chance I made my views very clear to a rather sheepish Jonathan. He was still sore about Henry Burrows' April Fool and claimed he was doing what he thought was best. "Yes," I stressed, "for yourself but not the churches. The idea of using churchwardens might be a good one, but only if they're given some training."

I also told Jonathan I knew he was a very dedicated pastor. I'd heard from one admirer how he'd spent many hours with one family sorting out a problem. While this was to be admired, he was wrong in thinking it was more important than taking services. He'd failed to get the balance right. It's not one or the other. Churchgoers are usually among the first to help their neighbours when in need. Worship and service go together. Jonathan listened quietly to what I said, but I couldn't be sure he was taking it in.

The first Sunday I was back at work I took services in three of my churches, each one attended by small, dispirited congregations. They complained how first they were expected to travel miles each Sunday to a distant church. Then back in their own churches they had to listen to churchwardens stumbling through long sermons read from a book which nobody understood.

It soon became clear I'd returned to work before I was ready. A month or two later I was still far from well. The bishop came to see me and suggested I consider retiring. I was glad to have the chance to tell him how I felt about the goings on during my absence. He listened carefully and said how pleased he was that Jonathan was learning by his mistakes. He then reminded me that caring for parishes is always a responsibility the clergy shared with their bishop and that I must have enough faith to leave things in his hands. There was something in the way he looked at me which suggested he knew more than he was letting on.

It felt strange announcing my retirement, almost like announcing the date of my death.

"Twill be that 'Opkins now." Peter Eastridge declared. "Snuffling 'is way round the parishes and putting everyone's back up."

I wondered what the bishop really had in mind. Almost thirty years ago the then bishop had used me in his experiment to bring new life to sleepy country parishes by joining them together. Did the present bishop want to try a different experiment on my parishes?

I had given plenty of notice in the hope the bishop might be able to find a successor. To leave all six parishes with a long vacancy might well destroy all I had achieved. As is the custom, I could play no part in selecting my successor. The only thing I could do was prepare the parishes for whatever came next.

In fact some good had come out of Jonathan's clumsy tactics. His actions had certainly made everyone wake up. I pointed out to the bishop the need to train lay worship leaders and he agreed to organise a course. Simon Williams, although a busy farmer, was making noises about training. So was Tom Stride, who had recently brought new life into the church at South Monkton. 'Ban-the-Bomb Stan', now painfully aware of his nickname, also applied, although he had been told in no uncertain terms to express his views in a much more balanced way. Mabel Waterhead joined Sonia Williams on a week-end course for youth workers. With all this going on I knew Jonathan would not be getting everything his own way.

Rumours continued to spread. First my successor was going to be a high churchman who would insist that everybody called him 'father'. Then, by accident, Annie Cook had evidently met a clergyman looking round Ashenridge Church who declared he had no use for bellringers, harvest festivals or any form of traditional country life. One day Will Swift met a possible candidate who openly declared he would use the old Prayer Book and nothing else in church.

In my last few weeks in office the mood seemed to change. Everyone went quiet. Nobody asked me any more questions. There were no more wild theories about my successor. Had the bishop brow-beaten them into accepting Jonathan Hopkins?

One day as I emerged from the vestry I overheard Peter Eastridge saying to Annie: "At least we knows a bit about 'im." I asked him who he was talking about. After a short pause he mentioned a builder who had apparently been looking at a couple of leaks coming from the church roof. This did not sound at all convincing and in his haste Peter pointed to a part of the roof that had only recently been repaired. When pressed he could not even remember the name of the builder.

I related all of this to Mary, but she tried to change the subject saying I must leave it in the hands of God. As Harry had once said, if the worst came to the worst, whoever was appointed would learn by his mistakes.

There was little I could do. I hoped with all my heart that Harry was right.

Chapter 17

Fine Rector Us's Lost

The first time I visited Ashenridge it was a sunny October morning. Today it looked much as it did then. The sun was shining. Scarlet apples smiled at me from gardens and orchards. Another season's Virginia creeper blazed in all its glory from the ancient walls, and crops of golden corn had been safely gathered in. On the surface nothing seemed to have changed and for a moment I wondered if I was in the middle of a dream. Would I wake up and discover I was back in the 1950s, being warned by my dark-suited contemporaries not to bury myself in the countryside?

The sound of the church bells and the noise of the traffic brought me back to reality. The village hall car park was nearly full; others had parked their vehicles bumper to bumper in the centre of the village.

The bells stopped ringing as I went for the last time to my familiar old stall. Was this really the last service I would take at Ashenridge Church? Mary sat in the front pew with Ann, Harry and the twins. Uncle Tiddly, wearing a loud check jacket and a bright-yellow bow tie, sat alongside them, clutching a box of man-size tissues. I sincerely hoped there wouldn't be any tears because it wouldn't take much to set me off. A quick glance told me that every parish was well represented and then I spotted the Methodists and the folk from Mill Chapel. There wasn't a spare seat to be had and for Jim Stillman and his pals from the Coach and Horses and several others it was standing room only at the back of the church.

With no qualified musician to train them our choir may not have been what it once was, but nevertheless the singing was superb. Sonia had recently taught Mabel to play the guitar and a group of youngsters gathered around them to form a small music group. That evening they put on their first performance. The Sunday School children let rip with their favourite choruses.

Will Swift and Henry Burrows led parts of the service, and 'Ban-the-Bomb Stan' and Simon Williams read the lessons.

It was time for me to address everyone for the last time. I wanted to give thanks to God for all that had happened over the years, and to express my heartfelt gratitude to everyone for their kindness, support and understanding. I intended to talk about the happy and sometimes dramatic times we had shared, and finally to point to the future with confidence. I'd rehearsed my words over and over again and knew exactly what I was going to say, yet despite all my preparation there was no accounting for the unexpected. It came in the form of a little girl, aged about seven, who was sitting in one of the pews below the pulpit. I didn't recognise her, but I did recognise her mother who years ago had been a member of our youth club. She listened carefully as I talked about some of the confusing messages I'd received over the years. I recalled how I'd once turned up in the wrong village to open a fête. There was laughter all round, but the little girl simply flicked her pigtails and glared at me.

I recounted another occasion when I'd nearly named a baby boy with a girl's name at a baptism. Again, everyone laughed, but I could see the little girl was not amused.

I concluded by saying that I'd even got in a muddle over this evening's service and it was only thanks to Mary that I'd arrived on time.

This proved too much for the little girl. She stood up and with a voice surprisingly penetrating for someone so small cried out: "Mr Longfield, you are a very naughty man. My teacher at school says that it is very rude to be late. You should not make people laugh about it."

Now, of course, everyone did just that, which eased things for me and took all the tension out of my farewell address. I could see the poor mother doing her best to explain things to her daughter, who evidently got the message because as I stepped down from the pulpit she rushed up and gave me a big kiss!

After the service I was hoping to have a chance to shake everyone by the hand, to thank them for their 'good luck' and 'happy retirement' cards, but Annie Cook and Peter Eastridge insisted I lead the whole company into the parish hall promising I'd have plenty of time to talk to one and all later on.

Mathilda Pink was already standing in the doorway and in an excited voice asked that we follow her into the hall. The floral decorations were of such a high standard that for a moment Mary and I wondered if she had employed a professional florist. Then we noticed vases of all shapes and sizes, even a few jam jars, had been put to good use. Seeing our warm reaction Mrs Pink blushed, her cheeks matching the deep-pink heads of the gorgeous chrysanthemums. She was quick to point out that this was not all her own work and that she'd been given plenty of help from other members of the WI.

Two long trestle tables were laden with a delicious-looking buffet. We guessed, correctly, that dear Annie and a few of her friends were responsible for this. I was finding it difficult to make myself heard above the din, but I did manage to say grace and seconds later the evening was well and truly under way.

Len Cooksley waved to me from the other side of the hall. I couldn't have missed him in his vivid blue jacket.

"Look, rector, I got this 'ere jacket for your do. Cost me 40p. 'Tis all spekerty." He held out both arms and the sleeves were indeed speckled with dashes of red, orange and yellow. Where on earth had he found it?

"Len, you look terrific."

Leaning towards me he chortled: "Funny thing, rector. There's me with me 'arthuritis' and you with yer tricky dicky. No, wait a minute, yer dricky ticky. 'Ang on, I'll get there in a minute. Got it, yer dicky ticker. And you'll soon be movin' to yer cottage. Reckon you've 'eard I'm on the move too. Annie's been naggin' me for years 'bout 'er spare room. 'Twill be nice to 'ave a bit o' company."

There it was, the sound of Max Malakhov's cowboy boots clip-clopping on the wooden floor   I'd been looking out for him because Mary and I wanted to say a special thank you for the surprise retirement gift he'd left at the rectory earlier in the day – a superb oil painting of Ashenridge Church.

"Hello, Max. Sorry we missed you this morning. What a wonderful surprise. We love the painting and know exactly where we're going to hang it at Greenbank Cottage. It'll bring back so many happy memories every time we look at it."

Max grasped me warmly by the hand. "You're welcome, Jack. You know, you and Mary have been the best neighbours anyone could have hoped for. I'm truly sad that you're leaving." Max gave me a quizzical look. "And talking about memories. You must have enough to last you a lifetime. Why don't you write a book about them?"

Peter Eastridge invited us to join him on the stage where representatives from the Badger Group had gathered to say a few words. One member felt he could not end his speech without telling a joke.

"I promise it's only a quick one, but just right for this evening. It goes like this. In Ashenridge, a frightened man ran into the Coach and Horses and shouted: 'Does anyone here own a big black dog with a white collar?' When no one answered he said: 'Oh dear, I think I've run over your vicar'."

It may only have been a short joke but it brought plenty of laughter and a long round of applause.

I was deeply touched when Roy Edwards, Cedric Palmer and Tim Ashman presented me with a beautiful leather-bound Bible on behalf of my previous fellow clergy. I expressed my heartfelt thanks and added jokingly: "I'd like to have thanked Harry Browne too, but where is he?" I could not quite understand why the whole room exploded into uncontrollable laughter.

Peter Eastridge was no public speaker but he was determined to put his feelings into words, saying that for many years he had misjudged me but had gradually seen my true worth. It was touching stuff.

"When you fust comed I used to shrug my shoulders and say 'fine rector us's got'. Now 'tis all different. What I says now, and what I means now is, 'fine rector us's lost'."

I turned to Peter and thanked him. What a wonderful feeling, the sudden realisation that my one-time critic had become a true friend.

He waited for everyone to settle down before drawing my attention to a large object on one side of the stage which he asked the twins to uncover. Mary and I were rendered speechless as a magnificent garden seat came into view.

From the foot of the stage Annie pointed to it. "We had that made specially for you. We wanted it to remind you of all your friends every time you sit on it. We're all going to miss you, it won't be the same ever again, and..." Poor Annie was close to tears and had to break off in mid-sentence.

It was then that Mary and I noticed the bronze plaque affixed to the top of the seat: Presented to Jack and Mary Longfield – In Grateful Thanks for 30 Years of Dedication and Service – October 1986.

Will caught hold of Mary's hand and pressed an envelope into it. "We had quite a bit of money left over so we thought you could use this to buy something else for your garden at Greenbank."

I was so overwhelmed I sat down with a jolt on the garden seat and Mary did likewise. I couldn't hold back the tears any longer.

"Grandad, what's wrong? Don't you like the seat?" Georgina had such a worried look on her face.

Matthew came and sat beside me. "Grandad, why are you crying? Are you sad?"

"Grandma and I love the garden seat, and yes, we are a bit sad, but let's call it happy sad. We're sad to be leaving, but happy, truly happy, for having had so many wonderful years in Ashenridge, at the church, and at the rectory. We'll cherish our memories. The whole Badger Group has played such a special part in our lives. We'll never forget you."

Without realising it, what had begun as a few words to Matthew had turned into an impromptu speech. After the applause there was a strange pause, almost as though everyone was waiting for something else to happen. I wondered whether I should break the silence by stepping down from the stage, but Uncle Tiddly suddenly threw his arms in the air. "Come on everyone," he yelled. "Three cheers for Jack and Mary Longfield. Hip hip hooray, hip hip hooray, hip hip hooray." The noise was deafening.

Will moved to the front of the stage and asked that everyone remain silent. He looked directly at me and speaking slowly, and with a fair amount of emotion in his voice, said: "Jack, there's something you should know. The bishop understands you have been anxious about the future of your six parishes. Before you go he wants you to meet the new rector of the Badger Group."

My heart missed a beat. This was the last thing I'd expected because it is rare for a successor to be named before an incumbent leaves. I'd only ever seen it happen once. Had Jonathan Hopkins somehow won the bishop round? Deep down I knew that Jonathan was a good man, but his beliefs about the future of the parishes were so out of tune with mine and those of the parishioners he would never be right for the job. I put on a brave face and steeled myself for the worst.

A jubilant Will caught hold of me by the shoulders and turned me until I was facing a small door on one side of the stage. I looked over my shoulder at Mary. She was shaking with emotion. Ann was shaking too.

"Why don't you open it," Will suggested. He had the strangest look on his face.

Trembling, I turned the handle and the door slowly creaked open. A figure ducked through the tiny gap and I found myself staring at a mop of unruly hair. My laughter and tears became one as a heavenly mixture of happiness and relief swept over me. The new rector of the Badger Group was standing before me.

It was Harry!